Best wishes to Ann & Earl
from
Joyce & Felix

All about the
Bearded Collie

All about the Bearded Collie

JOYCE COLLIS

PELHAM BOOKS

First published in Great Britain by
PELHAM BOOKS LTD
44 Bedford Square
London WC1B 3DP
1979
Revised edition published 1985

British Library Cataloguing in Publication Data

Collis, Joyce
    All about the bearded collie.—Rev. ed.
    1. Bearded collie
    I. Title
    636.7′3   SF429.B32

   ISBN 0-7207-1615-2

Typeset, printed and bound by
Butler & Tanner Ltd, Frome and London

Contents

Illustrations

Photographs

Figures

Table

Photographic Credits

C.M. Cooke 41
Fox Photos 6
F.E. Garwood (Dog World) 11–17, 22, 26–36, 40, 43, 46, 49
Diane Pearce 47

The line diagrams are by Margaret Lewis (1-6 and 11) and Tony Mould.

Foreword

It is one of the wonders of the world of dogs that the undoubted charms and obvious claims to a high place in the poll of popularity of the Bearded Collie remained undiscovered for so long.

Beardies, as all owners and admirers know, have almost all the virtues of the ideal friend of man. Their long shaggy coats can be a bit of a nuisance if not properly cared for – but what other being, human or otherwise, has only one fault?

Cheerful, extrovert, abounding with energy but full of a confiding sweetness of character that would charm the rooks out of the trees, they would undoubtedly be my first choice among all canines if I were not a life-long addict of other smooth-coated breeds.

It is a pleasure to meet them, and a privilege to judge them. The breed is almost uniquely free of any important fault. It is often a sad business to have to choose between a ringful of beautiful specimens, differing only in the development of their coats or the shade of colour in their eyes. One has a feeling of being grossly unfair to the many who cannot be given a prize, which are equally worthy, but just not as ready for the particular occasion as those at the top of the line.

A modern trend to over-present the Beardie will I hope be severely dealt with by the powers in the breed clubs. The Beardie must not degenerate into a hair dresser's dummy, but must be kept as the good-looking, well made working dog that he is, still capable of the herding work for which he was evolved.

Joyce Collis has done a splendid job in writing this book on the breed. That she is a successful breeder and exhibitor, and, more important, a true lover of Beardies, comes through in every chapter. I cannot do more than recommend the book to everyone interested in the Beardie, and wish it all the luck it deserves.

TOM HORNER

Acknowledgements

I would like to express my grateful thanks to my husband, without whose help in feeding and looking after the dogs we would not be able to go to so many shows.

My sincere thanks go to Mr Felix Cosme, who took over completely the running of the kennels while I wrote this book; without his advice and help this book would never have been written.

Miss Margaret Lewis kindly and expertly contributed several line drawings.

Mr Frank Garwood took the excellent photographs taken specially for this book. I would also like to thank the many kind friends who allowed me to use photographs of their dogs.

Preface to the Revised Edition

I am so pleased to have been able to revise *All About the Bearded Collie*. So much has happened in our breed in the last five years, that the alterations and additions have been many. Sadly a few of the dogs mentioned in the earlier book have died, and only sad memories remain of much loved companions. I have included in the chapter on The History of the Breed, photographs of dominant Beardies who have made their mark and have produced strong types. Many are not top winners, but nevertheless are excellent specimens with the typical Bearded Collie character.

The colours of our dogs is a challenging subject, queried by so many, understood by so few. The shades of coat colour from birth to adulthood is wide and varied, making it a fascinating breed to own.

In Chapter 3, I have extended the sections on Buying a Puppy as a Pet, and Buying a Puppy for Show, and also added further information in the chapter on Training – this is by popular demand.

I sincerely thank all those who have complimented me on the first edition of this book. My aim originally was to cater for the newcomer to the breed and the novice, and from reports that I have received from owners here and abroad, that purpose has been achieved with great success.

Again I must thank my partner Felix Cosme, who has helped with checking the manuscript and given invaluable advice on training.

JC

1 The History of the Breed

There has always been conjecture concerning the beginnings of the Bearded Collie. Search as you may, you can find only scraps of information. But the basic origin of the Breed cannot be doubted. The shepherds and drovers of Scotland and the North of England needed a dog that could stand for hours guarding their flocks, but it had also to be one built for speed and stamina. Living in the wildest country, he would have to have a warm undercoat and harsh topcoat to keep him in good health in the bitter climate. The farmers had worked and bred animals all their lives, and by selective breeding, whether with a sheepdog strain from overseas or a mixture of Scottish Deerhound and Collie, they bred this hardy working-type dog for their daily companion, without ever considering keeping records of any sort. They would not have bothered whether their dogs had the correct Collie markings or followed any particular standard. They must have followed a pattern however, to some extent, as the Beardie has mainly bred true to type, and, most important of all, the typical Beardie characteristics are predominant in their descendants: although lively and active, they are trainable, and their boisterousness is usually because they are so willing to please; most are blessed with that typical Bearded Collie 'far-seeing' expression.

Old photographs show Beardies as very rough-looking animals, high on leg, with very little coat; what coat there is looks harsh. They were noticeably light-boned, and so different from the present day show Bearded Collie as sometimes to look like another breed. I love the description of the Beardie of far-off days: 'Shaggy-haired, large-headed, large-eyed, big-nostrilled sheepdogs, unkempt-looking with coats like untidy doormats.'

Confusion must also arise when tracing the history of a breed which is referred to by so many names; Coalie (named either for the black-faced sheep they herded, or for their own black colour), Highland Colley, Scottish Highland Colley, Sheepdog, Drover's dog, Scottish Bearded Collie.... Only quite recently has the Breed been called solely the Bearded Collie, because of his lovely fall of beard.

Mrs R. Lee mentions the Sheepdog in her book *Anecdotes of the Habits and Instinct of Animals* written in 1854:

'... long, lanky, rough-haired, with drooping bushy tail; long ears, half erect; long sharp muzzle; black and fulvous [reddish-yellow] in

'Mr J. Dalgliesh's
Bearded Collie.'
From *The New Book
of the Dog*.

'Lord Arthur Cecil's
Bearded Collie Ben.'
From *The New Book
of the Dog*.

colour, often mingled with white; the Shepherd's dog yields to none
in fidelity and sagacity. In his own peculiar calling, nothing can
exceed his vigilance, his quick comprehension and his intimate
knowledge of every individual entrusted to his care. Rushing into
the middle of his flock, he singles out any one member of it and
brings it to his master. Fierce in his defence of all, he keeps them
together by incessantly prowling round them, dragging the wan-
derers back to their companions and fiercely attacking those who
would offer them an injury. At night he guides them to their fold;
and if this should be in an exposed situation he throws himself
across the entrance, so that the intruding enemy will have to pass
over his body to commence his work of destruction.'

If one has to imagine the original Beardie, this surely could be his
epitaph. Another reference made about a shepherd's Scottish Sheepdog well known to the author of this book is:

'I know a shepherd who praises his dog as beyond comparison, the
best dog and worker he ever owned. [The dog] was of a surly
unsociable temper, disdaining flattery and refusing all caresses. His
love of his master and attention to all his commands and wishes
will never again be equalled by any other of the canine race. He
had been bought in a market for a guinea, an enormous sum in the
year 1844. He was scarcely a year old and had had no training, but
as soon as he discovered that it was his duty to learn, he worked
with an eagerness and will that bespoke a great share of the reasoning faculty.'

Left on his own, a Sheepdog or Collie will reason and work with
great intelligence and initiative; he has inherited the ability to creep
up with trance-like attention and face the flock, encouraging them to

move without stampeding. It is sad to think that some, through their close association with man, have lost this ability, because they have lost their independence and therefore very seldom if ever use their own reasoning powers. They would be helpless if left to fend for themselves more than a few weeks. The dog, formerly wild, has surrendered his freedom and conquered his instinct to enter into the position of friendship between man and beast.

About 1880 the large estates in northern Britain were broken up into small holdings and the extensive forests sub-divided into limited shootings – stalking deer was going out of fashion. One famous experienced deer stalker of that time, Cameron of Locknield, soberly put the question, 'Ought dogs to be used in the forest at all?' Admitting that the Deerhound was helpful in tracking, he went on to discuss the breed best adapted for the sport. With a Highlander's love for the Deerhound he reluctantly decided that those magnificent dogs were not the most suitable for the smaller estates; he continued,

'For use on the hill nothing beats the Highland Collie; he is possessed of instinct – one may almost call it a sense – in a higher degree than any other breed, and he is more tractable; he will run by sight or by scent, loose or on a cord; he will keep close to his master requiring no ghillie to lead him; he can be taught to lie down, and will even learn to crawl when necessary, and at any rate his motions are those of an animal who knows that he is trying to approach a prey unobserved. But the chief merit in a collie, over all other dogs for following a wounded deer, consists of his wonderful faculty for distinguishing between the track of a wounded and that of a cold stag.'

The spread of dog shows and dog showing had little by little en-

Unnamed Beardie on a post card of 1919.

A postcard of the mid-1920s.

gulfed breed after breed, but in the 1920s it had not as yet reached the far northern counties. Shepherds and their working sheepdogs did not as yet know or care about this pastime; they did not worry that their dogs had matted coats so long as they could work and do all that was asked of them. In *The New Book of the Dog* James C. Dalgliesh has written extensively about the Collie. Writing about the Bearded Collie, he says that he considered Peebleshire as the true home of the Beardie; Sir Walter Thorburn and other patrons of the breed had for long contributed prizes at the annual pastoral show in that country for the best Bearded Collie owned by shepherds, and they were very well filled classes.

Balmacneil Scott, as illustrated in *Hutchinson's Dog Encyclopaedia* in the mid-1930s. The caption reads: 'This is a good example of the Highland Collie, winner at the Scottish Kennel Club and Ladies' Kennel Association Shows, owned by Mrs Cameron Miller. Observe the remarkable coat.'

Gradually the shepherds had decided that they would enter their dogs in local shows, and not only would they breed Beardies for brains and working capabilities, but also breed to compete against other dogs. In the standard they adopted, many points were given for good legs and feet, bone and body, while head was not of such importance. At this time, about 1925, there were one or two attempts to start up clubs, but very little was heard of the Beardie in the show-rings until Mrs Cameron Miller started breeding and showing her Balmacneil stock in 1930-9. Her dogs, Balmacneil Scott, Balmacneil Rork and Balmacneil Jock, were very impressive-looking dogs; all show a good length of straight, profuse coat, strong bone, and look more like the present day Beardie.

One or two breeders kept going through the war years, as shown by reports of Bearded Collies being found in outlying parts of the country filtering in. Mr Sidney Green, of the Swalehall prefix, remembers a blue-black Beardie (origin unknown) in 1940. Another typical fawn dog, farm-bred, was owned by Mr Green, but it could not be registered then as there was no Kennel Club classification. This dog lived to the mid '50s. Mr Green was so impressed with the breed that he searched everywhere for another; finally he heard of Mrs Willison of Bothkennar, who was breeding Shetland Sheepdogs and Bearded Collies. Meanwhile a friend of his saw an advertisement in *Exchange & Mart*: 'Suit to fit man; would give Bearded Collie bitch in exchange.' Mr Green wasted no time in answering the advertisement, taking not a suit but money to Castle Bolton in Wensleydale, Yorkshire. In his own words, 'Here on arrival I saw a

Miss Barbara Donague (now Iremonger) with the Bothkennar dogs. From left to right, they are: Buskie, Peter (at rear), Bruce, Jeannie, Baidh, Bawbee, Bailie.

beautiful black-and-white Beardie, Fly of Swalehall; black body, and white paws, face and tail-tip. After haggling with the Bailiff of Bolton Castle, I was able to purchase her for £7. I then wrote to Mrs Willison and she invited me to bring the bitch to Sandy Lodge. She was very impressed with her, and before long Fly of Swalehall was registered with the Kennel Club.' The tragic loss of the bitch from distemper upset Mr and Mrs Green's plans to found a kennel of Bearded Collies. Later another bitch was found, sable and white, registered as Swalehall Kitty Norton. She is the ancestor of some of our present day Champions. She was duly mated to a Bothkennar dog, Bruce of Bothkennar, and produced nine puppies.

No chapter on the history of the Bearded Collie would be complete unless the famous Bothkennar owner and breeder was mentioned. Mrs Willison was living at Bothkennar Grange, Middlesex, when her first Beardie (later registered Jeannie of Bothkennar) came into her possession; she considered her the most obedient dog she had ever owned; without any training Jeannie could work all kinds of livestock – poultry, sheep, cattle, and even obstinate goats. It was because of Jeannie's wonderful qualities, her intelligence and her endearing nature, that she felt she must perpetuate her strain; she set about trying to find a mate for her. After years of searching, with many disappointments, she found the dog that was to be registered as Bailie of Bothkennar. The mating took place in 1950; the four whelps she kept were Bogle, Bravado, Bruce and the bitch Buskie; this was her foundation stock.

Bearded Collies, 1912.

2 The Breed Standard

The Standard has been vastly improved since the very short unofficial standard drawn up in 1912, which stated: 'A variant of the Pastoral breed is known in Scotland, the Bearded Collie, who differs chiefly by reason that his coat is less woolly, and that he is in possession of a tail, the amputation of which in the Southern variety is a recognised custom in England.'

In *Dogs since 1900* (written in 1950), there is a paragraph about the Bearded Collie, but no Standard. The author continues:

'Mrs Cameron Miller showed a few in London between the wars without gaining any recruits, and since 1925 one or two have appeared. They have more suggestion of the Old English Sheepdog than of the Collie, but they do not carry the wealth of coat of the former, although they are rough and shaggy, with hair on the legs down to the feet. A slate or reddish fawn is the usual colour, sometimes with a white collar or white on the legs. A beard under the chin gives the name. The tail is undocked. In size they are somewhat smaller than the Bobtail. No official standard has been formulated.'

The caption under the pictures of the Bearded Collies being shown by Mrs Cameron Miller states, 'The Bearded Collie can quite easily be mistaken for the Old English Sheepdog. This is Balmacneil Rork, a great prize-winner, the property of Mrs Cameron Miller.' The other picture shows an even larger dog called Balmacneil Scott; the caption states, 'This is a good example of the Highland Collie, a winner at the Scottish Kennel Club and Ladies' Kennel Association Shows, owned by Mrs Cameron Miller. Observe the remarkable coat. The size and coat show a remarkable resemblance to the Old English Sheepdog.'

In *About our Dogs*, written by Croxton Smith earlier (in 1931), is a little more about the breed:

'Superficially it may be said that the Bearded Collie of Scotland, and the Old English Sheepdog have a good deal of resemblance to one another. No doubt they have, but there are differences which separate them very distinctly. Both have shaggy coats, but the Scottish dog is smaller, not so strong in muzzle, has a small beard under his chin, and his tail is not docked. He gives the impression of being able to move easily and to spend long hours in his work. The eye, roundish in shape, is very expressive, denoting a high order of intelligence. The colour varies, but dark hazel is preferred.

'I should have thought that it was possible to find a fair number of Bearded Collies at work in Scotland, but Miss Augusta Bruce told me in 1930 that they had become extremely scarce, and that Mrs Cameron Miller, Balmacneil, Perthshire, who was trying to found a kennel, had found it difficult to get typical dogs. I realised that when I happened to be judging them a few weeks later at the Ladies' Kennel Association show. None of the other exhibited could compare with Balmacneil Scott, who was really a delightful dog in every way. There is no official Standard for the Bearded Collie.'

The mention of the Bearded Collie each time in these early Standards is usually followed up immediately with reference to the similarity in some respects to the Old English Sheepdog; many of the early photos of that breed could indeed be taken for the Bearded Collie, not only the olden-day Bearded Collie, but even some of the modern day specimens.

One writer gives the description, 'It is an active dog, very strongly made, but not as heavy and four-square as the Old English Sheepdog.... The head should be fairly large and square with plenty of space for brain, but should not resemble the Old English Sheepdog....'

The similarities do not end at the size of the head, or when the dog stands four-square, so the Standard of the Bearded Collie should make it very apparent that the Beardie is a breed on its own; anything that could give the impression of resembling in any way the Old English Sheepdog – or for that matter the Border Collie – should be corrected in detail.

A Standard was passed by the K.C. in 1964, and the one approved in 1978 shows a great improvement on the early one. Although the 1978 Standard is only a clarification, it does give more detail and description of the requirements of the Breed. We are at present in the process of getting a revised re-write of the Bearded Collie Standard and I have included it here. The date of the re-write is 13 March 1984 and I am sure that it will be some months before the final draft is published – it could well contain more amendments too. Personally I feel that an even more comprehensive description should have been included, so that the Standard did not leave such a wide margin for misunderstanding and misinterpretation when translated into other languages. When sentences have ambiguous meanings, there is too much latitude for foreigners to alter and misinterpret; in many overseas countries the Bearded Collie has become a very popular breed, winning Best in Show and the Working Group, so that judges who have never shown an interest in the Bearded Collie are now being confronted for the first time with top quality specimens that can hold their own with the best in the final line-up.

Coat seems to be the main problem; the cosmetically presented Beardie with the coat to the ground does not comply with the Standard, but the wording does not make it a fault. 'Length and density of hair sufficient to provide a protective coat and to enhance shape of dog, but not enough to obscure natural lines of the body.' If the coat is body-hugging, it will not obscure the lines of the body even though it might reach the ground. The increase in length of coat towards the chest could be due to a terrific length from cheeks and chin. In the States the U.S. Kennel Club has formulated an interpretation of the last British Standard; but it has added an even more comprehensive list of the requirements, considering the British one to be ambiguous and in some respects incomplete.

Most of the British Standard is clear to us British breeders, who have for years worked on less, and the Bearded Collie has always been with us, although gradually changing before our eyes, so what we take for granted, others on first encountering the breed could be confused and unsure of the finer points.

One example of the American tendency to specify in detail is height. The general pattern of dogs and bitches in the rings do come within the 21–2 in. for dogs, and 20–21 in. for bitches. A half-inch either way would not be so noticeable, or penalised, as the large classes in the adult range show that breeders do mainly stick to within the Standard. The Americans mention the fact that the size they require is for *adult* dogs and bitches, obviously allowing for less size in the Puppy and Junior Classes. This gives the judge the question whether to penalise an up-to-size Junior; but who is to say that this Junior has not stopped growing and will yet go over size? I prefer to judge height with the British Standard in mind; 'Overall quality and proportions should be considered before size, but excessive variation from the ideal height should be discouraged.'

Revised re-write of the Bearded Collie Standard (*13 March 1984*)

Characteristics. Alert, lively, self confident and active.
General Appearance. Lean active dog, longer than it is high in an approximate proportion of 5–4, measured from point of chest to point of buttock. Bitches may be slightly longer. Though strongly made, should show plenty of daylight under body and should not look too

heavy. Bright, enquiring expression is a distinctive feature.

Temperament. Steady, intelligent working dog, with no signs of nervousness or aggression.

Head and Skull. Head in proportion to size. Skull broad, flat and square, distance between stop and occiput being equal to width between orifices of ears. Muzzle strong and equal in length to distance between stop and occiput. Whole effect being that of a dog with strength of muzzle and plenty of brain room. Moderate stop. Nose large and square, generally black but normally following coat colour in blues and browns. Nose and lips of solid colour without spots or patches. Pigmentation of lips and eye rims follows nose colour.

Eyes. Toning with coat colour, set widely apart and large, soft and affectionate, not protruding. Eyebrows arched up and forward but not so long as to obscure eyes.

Ears. Ears of medium size and drooping. When alert, ears lift at base, level with, but not above top of skull, increasing apparent breadth of skull.

Mouth. Teeth large and white, scissor bite preferred. Neither undershot nor overshot.

Neck. Moderate length, muscular and slightly arched.

Forequarters. Shoulders sloping well back. Legs straight and vertical with good bone, covered with shaggy hair all round. Pasterns flexible without weakness.

Body. Length of back comes from length of ribcage and not that of loin. Back level and ribs well sprung but not barrelled. Loins strong and chest deep, giving plenty of heart and lung room.

Hindquarters. Well muscled with good second thighs, well bent stifles and low hocks. Lower leg falls at a right angle to ground and, in normal stance, is just behind a line vertically below point of buttocks.

Feet. Oval in shape with soles well padded. Toes arched and close together, well covered with hair including between pads.

Tail. Set low, without kink or twist, and long enough for end of bone to reach at least point of hock. Carried low with an upward swirl at tip whilst standing or walking, may be extended at speed. Never carried over back. Covered with abundant hair.

Gait/Movement. Supple, smooth and long reaching, covering ground with minimum of effort.

Coat. Double with soft, furry and close undercoat. Outer coat flat, harsh, strong and shaggy, free from woolliness and curl, though slight wave permissible. Length and density of hair sufficient to provide a protective coat and to enhance shape of dog, but not enough to obscure natural lines of body. Coat must not be trimmed in any way. Bridge of the nose sparsely covered with hair slightly longer on side just to cover lips. From cheeks, lower lips and under chin, coat increases in length towards chest, forming typical beard.

Colour. Slate grey, reddish fawn, black, blue, all shades of grey, brown and sandy, with or without white markings. When white occurs it appears on foreface, as a blaze on skull, on tip of tail, on chest, legs and feet and, if round the collar, roots of white hair should not extend behind shoulder. White should not appear above hocks on outside of hind legs. Slight tan markings are acceptable on eyebrows, inside ears, on cheeks, under root of tail, and on legs where white joins main colour.

Size. Ideal height: Dogs 53–56 cm (21–22 ins). Bitches 51–53 cm (20–21 ins). Excessive variation from ideal height should be discouraged, but overall quality and proportions should be considered before size.

Faults. Any departure from the foregoing points should be considered a fault and the seriousness with which the fault is regarded should be in exact proportions to its degree.

Note. Male animals should have two apparently normal testicles fully descended into the scrotum.

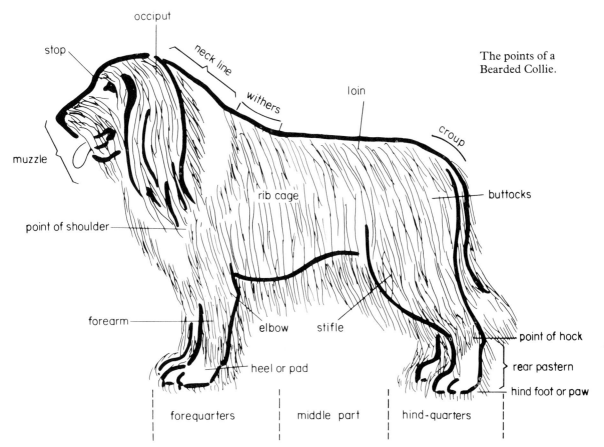

The points of a Bearded Collie.

The Beardie on the move should hold a good topline, with tail held at the correct level.

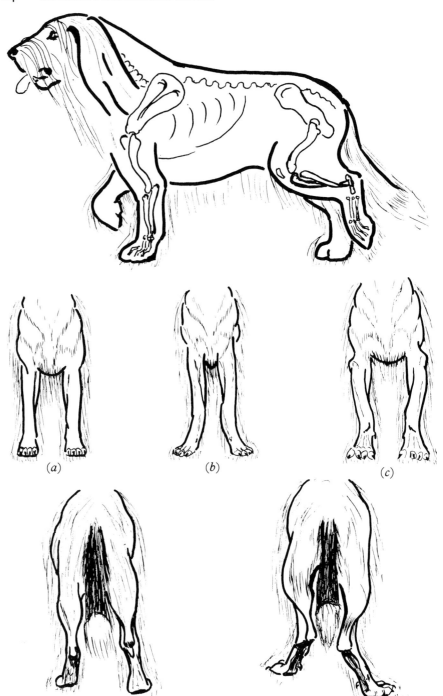

Correct and incorrect fronts: (*a*) is excellent; (*b*) is 'east and west', with pinched elbows, and is too narrow; (*c*) is barrel-legged, with loaded shoulders and poor feet.

(*a*) (*b*) (*c*)

The correct hind-quarters (left), compared to cow-hocked ones (right).

Markings: (*a*) and (*b*) are correct, although (*a*) does not have the full white collar. (*b*) comes just into the limits of what is acceptable, since the white follows the shoulder line and does not go behind it.

Markings, continued: (*c*) is another correct Beardie marking, although there is no white collar or blaze, and the muzzle has the minimum of white marking. (*d*) is not correct, since the marking covers the head on one side only, and the other is white. If used for breeding, this dog could well be the progenitor of other mis-marked puppies.

(d)

(e)

Markings, continued: (e) and (f) are badly mis-marked, and should not be shown or bred from. (e) has too much white, and (f) has patchy white marks on the body. Even so, their construction and outline is excellent.

(f)

3 Buying a Puppy; Initial Care

Some owners will be happy to keep their Beardies simply as pets; others will plan all along to show and breed; still others may be interested in Obedience training (Beardies are particularly good at Obedience; that is why the Bearded Collie Club and the Southern Counties Bearded Collie Club have devised a series of Working Tests, which are fully explained in Appendix 2). (Of course, some people start as pet owners, but become interested in showing later.) These different would-be owners will therefore be looking for different things when they set out to buy a puppy.

THE BEARDED COLLIE AS A PET

Anyone wishing to own a companion dog of unsurpassable devotion could do no better than to choose a Bearded Collie. A Beardie will rapidly take his or her place as one of the family, and will show an intelligent understanding and acceptance of every situation.

Very few breeders aim to breed litters solely to sell as pets. Prospective buyers often do not understand that the main aim for any breeder is to produce litters of top-quality puppies; breeders must accept, though, that some puppies will be the top winners, others will not be so good. These latter are the ones sold as pets; they will be reared exactly as the rest of the litter, but will not have the desired show points that their more fortunate litter-mates will be endowed with. Things like even markings cannot be overlooked when a breeder will be competing against other top-quality dogs. Puppies picked out to be sold as pets may therefore be slightly mismarked, or unevenly marked, or have a high-set tail, or a tail that definitely kinks or is curled over the back. It could have small high-set ears. None of these faults will alter the fact that the puppy can be an ideal pet. When the coat grows, the show points on the body will be camouflaged, the ears will have long feathering so will not look so small. Colours will blend into each other so that it will be difficult to see where the colour ends and the white begins.

You must decide whether you want a dog or bitch. A dog is larger in size and height than a bitch; he is also a little harder to train. If there are lively young boys in the family the dog tends to join in all the rough games and if allowed to do this can become boisterous with children and not all children appreciate large hairy dogs. A bitch is much quieter and easier to train, but it must be taken into account that twice a year she will be in season, at which time she must be kept in strict confinement (especially if there are children around who are likely to leave gates and doors open allowing her to escape, or wandering amorously-intent dogs to visit her).

I have at times been asked for a bitch then informed that the new owner intends to have her spayed. Bitches are in great demand by the breeders, and even though I do not like to encourage bitch owners to breed litters indiscriminately I do think it is a waste of a well-bred bitch for her to be spayed before she has had a chance to prove her worth.

The temperament of a pet Beardie is very important. Normally the Beardie is a very healthy animal, and should live for fourteen to fifteen years. When an older person buys a Beardie they do not want to have to cope with a wild uncontrollable animal; there is no reason for a young dog to be allowed to get out of hand and early firm training will result in a rewarding companionship for many years.

Another consideration is that of colour. Beardies can be born brown, blue, fawn or black. The colour can change quite a lot as the dog grows, usually getting much lighter at first, then returning to the same colour as the hair on the ears. This rule applies to those Beardies born brown and white; the blue and fawn types stay very much the same shade throughout the dog's life. I mention these facts because even when the puppy is bought solely as a pet some buyers are very definite about the colour they want.

The Bearded Collie Puppy for Show
When you are picking a puppy with the intention of showing it, temperament again is a very important factor to take into account. We have seen top-quality show specimens refusing to be handled by the Judge, backing away and cringing to the ground. With all their super qualities what earthly good are these animals for stud or for show? The serious buyer should visit one or two shows. Go and see the Beardies in action; talk to the breeders. Ask questions. See the quality of the puppies that come regularly from particular kennels. Not just one or two but the breeders that have been breeding for many years and producing top-quality stock here and abroad. I say 'abroad' as Great Britain is the home of the Bearded Collie and people from overseas always prefer to come here for foundation stock, as they have done for many years. Find out which breeders have puppies. Read and learn all you can about the breed before deciding

which kennel or private owner will answer all your requirements. If a puppy is available, make an appointment to visit. If the sire and dam are there, ask to see them; you will be able to get an idea of the size, temperament and looks that your choice will have. You must understand though that the dam will be slightly wary and may even be nervous, carefully guarding her pups.

By visiting the dog's home you can tell about the way it is cared for, too. I have been amazed at the people who have bought a puppy from a private home – sometimes even from kennels – and then remarked on the filthy state of the place, the dirty surroundings the puppies were reared in, and the poor condition of the dam. Surely they can see for themselves that a puppy from such a place will not be free from worms and other parasites, and will not have been fed with the necessary good food to assist in its development. If I were not a busy kennel owner, I would suggest that you visit several breeders before making a final choice. However, from personal experience I know that kennel owners' time is limited; they do not have hours to spare for people 'doing the rounds'. Nevertheless, serious buyers are always welcome, and kennel owners *will* somehow find time to show their stock, and to discuss training, feeding and the welfare of their puppies.

When the puppy is young, it is very difficult to tell if some of the faults that you see will remain in the adult; white can blend into silver-grey or light brown, and with growth in the coat, markings can change drastically – even to show-winning standard; even, perfect markings are a bonus when the show puppy has all the other desired attributes. It would be so easy if you could surely pick a potential champion out of the litter; there are the occasional lucky ones who do this, and with all the luck in the world it has turned out as they had hoped. But it should be remembered that so many things can go wrong, even though a terrific amount of work has gone into planning the litter. I won't list all the heartbreaking faults that can appear; breeders of several litters will know them.

There is the other side of the coin too: a fair number of puppies have been sold as pets by knowledgeable breeders, and later turned out to be champions. Luck is the most important factor. Puppies go through an ugly stage, when you might regret your choice. I never mind an ugly stage, as I always know it cannot get worse only better – and usually I am right, the ugly duckling becomes a beautiful swan at about 18 months. Being a slow maturer we know that its best time will come at three years of age and then on until about seven when it becomes a veteran.

There are the pups that never look immature; they never seem to go through the gangling stage, are never out of coat and win Junior

Warrant points in next to no time, but many of those early winners seem to disappear from the show world before they become adults.

Eight weeks is usually the age at which puppies are picked; markings often seem to be given the most attention by novice buyers, but I would say that temperament, conformation, head (ear set and shape of skull and muzzle) outline, and stance should be noted before markings and colour.

Learn, read, watch, before making the final choice, remember that your dog will be living with you for possibly as many as fourteen years. There will be sacrifices to be made, but the joy you will receive from the companionship, love and loyalty of a Beardie will amply repay you. Whatever else you decide remember that, for showing or as a pet, the dog's most important quality is temperament. A bad-tempered or wild, unruly dog or bitch is no joy to live with, nor is a shy one.

We assess the litter daily, handling each puppy, talking to them the whole time so that they get to know our voices. This routine starts at four weeks; prior to that time the bitch resents intrusion so we just visit to feed her and see that all is well. At four weeks they are walking about; we take note of tail set, length of back, neck and head, at this age. It is so easy to assess a Beardie litter as with even the most similar markings there are slightly different patterns; also one litter can consist of the four different colours.

Let us forget markings and go deeply into the other points that we look for when picking out a show puppy. This is so much easier when you have actually bred the litter. In fact as the puppies are born some breeders take to one particular pup, and never change their minds. I prefer to wait until the pups are four weeks old, then spend hours watching and assessing. With a large litter there are so many to choose from, and that makes life easy; with a small litter, faults that you see but that can be altered by training must be taken into account. Where there are faults that cannot be altered by training, these puppies should be sold as pets. I take the puppy that I have chosen and place it on a table where it must stand foursquare, and while I handle it I expect it to wag its little tail in greeting. Forelegs must be straight with no ten-to-two stance. There should be a level topline, and I prefer a low-set tail that even at this age reaches to the hocks; I look for a good bend of stifle. I like to see the puppy with its head down eating its food or drinking from a dish and observe that it can have its head in the dish without bending its front legs; this means it has a good length of neck. The skull must be flat with nice big ears, set in the correct place, in fact a squarish head with the cheeks well defined.

I watch the puppies daily, and especially the one I have picked. I do not assess its show potential again until it is eight weeks, and then I have to make my final decision as the rest of the litter are due to go to their new homes. By this time the puppy will have developed a nice little hair rosette slightly obscuring its eyes, which by this age will have changed to match the colour of coat. If I am picking a brown puppy I part the coat on the back, and expect to see the dark brown colour going right down to the skin. If the colour pales noticeably in the parting, the coat is going to change to nearly white when it becomes a Junior, and if the eyes are lighter than the coat at that age they will remain light. I prefer to see a dark brown coat colour to the skin and nice dark brown eyes to match. The born-black puppy with the white markings will by this time have silver grey spectacles, silver showing on hocks and on the front of the legs, if it is from light grey, light brown, fawn or blue parents, and grandparents. The puppies that we have bred from born black that stay black lines do not have grey at all in their coat at this age or even as they grow to the Junior stage. They remain black and white only getting one or two grey hairs as they become veterans.

The pigmentation of the puppy's exposed skin should be of the correct colour, covering the nose and lips by eight weeks. We have had puppies with incomplete pigment up to ten weeks, but so long as it is noticeably covering the nose and lips we have had no problem with lack of it by the time the pup is twelve weeks old. The problems some owners have with pigment fading after several months is a completely different problem, and one that has been corrected with different remedies.

The puppy's movements cannot be assessed properly until it is past the staggering stage. The puppy with really good conformation is usually the best mover. With sound front, good length of back, correct bend of stifle, strong and correct hocks it should glide around.

PREPARING TO RECEIVE THE PUPPY

The part of your house that the puppy is to occupy should be prepared before he is taken home. A quiet corner in the kitchen, outhouse, or anywhere where his movements can be restricted during the night and part of the day, will be suitable. It is so unwise to allow a young untrained puppy to have complete freedom of the house. Very few doting parents would allow a small child to have access to every room, and yet so many owners allow their puppy to run riot through lounge, dining room, stairs and bedroom, and then complain bitterly about torn wallpaper, chewed up carpets and messed floors. I have no sympathy with them, but all with the puppy - but if the situation continues, there will be another Junior looking for a new home before long! So many owners forget that they are dealing with a young *animal*, not a human being; the puppy dog has the instincts and behaviour of an animal and should be expected to behave as such. He is not naughty if he wets or messes on the floor, or if he is bored after being shut up in a small room for a time and chews anything he can get hold of, or if he tries to mount your leg or steal food that has been left within each reach; he is behaving quite naturally and will continue to act in the only way he knows how, unless he is trained not to.

Beardie pups of a few days before their eyes have opened.

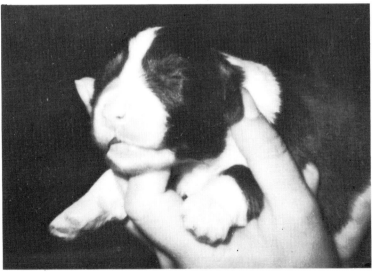

Six-week-old
puppies sired by
Suzanne Anderson's
Danish Int. Ch.
Østermarks
Chieftain out of
Vigsbjergs Yvette.

COLLECTING THE PUPPY

When you leave with your puppy, you should also have in your possession: its pedigree; a diet sheet so that you keep the diet the same (a change would affect the puppy's digestive system); all the Kennel Club papers (although these days you may not be able to have them immediately: K.C. papers used always to be returned to breeders in time for them to accompany the puppy when it was sold, but at present, processing can take three or four months, and you may have to have the papers forwarded later); a receipt for your money.

Should you have accepted the puppy on breeding terms, you should make very sure that you understand the agreement, and that it is registered with the Kennel Club. A 'breeding terms' agreement is one where the buyer of a bitch pays the breeder a down payment, and agrees to follow with 'payment in kind': one or more of the bitch's first litter. Make sure that you have a full agreement which covers all possible contingencies (the bitch may produce only one puppy, or may die), and explains who is to choose the sire, and so on.

Your puppy should be lively and active (but you must expect that it may be a little nervous on the journey, with all the new noises it will encounter). It should have a healthy and clean coat, ears, eyes and rear end. Its nails should be cut, and the breeder should be able to assure you that it has been wormed twice, and that it is completely weaned from its mother. (Consequently, it will be needing four meals a day, two milk and two meat. The diet sheet should give you details of exactly the amount it will eat, and the number of vitamin tablets which should be given with the meals.) You should also have information on grooming and training, and the telephone number of the breeder so that you can call (at reasonable hours) if you have any initial problems.

CAR JOURNEYS

It is best to let the puppy stay on the floor at the back of the car on his first journey, rather than on your lap, in case he is sick. (Put down lots of newspapers.) Subsequently, he should be trained to stay quietly on his own, either on the back seat or, in an estate car, behind the rack. If he is trained to do this from the start, then he will always expect to travel this way.

Stop any barking immediately. When he is a puppy, it may sound amusing, but laughter will encourage him to bark again and again, and when he is older, continual barking will not be quite so entertaining. It will be nerve-racking to have continual loud barking at every car, person or other dog that goes by. Train your dog to guard the car sensibly, but reprimand any barking firmly.

BEHAVIOUR AND TRAINING

The puppy will have been playing with his brothers and sisters for the first part of his life; their games will have included biting, play-growling and mounting. This play is only preparation for their adult life, and is instinctive practice; when they are deprived of dog companions and have to adjust to human companionship, who can blame them if the play continues on the same lines with their human owners? Firm but gentle chastisement will soon stop too boisterous a puppy from grabbing your leg or arm; only if it is continually repeated when he is older should you use a small roll of newspaper, either to hit him gently on his rump, or to make a big noise by hitting the floor beside him. Never allow any of his naughtiness to become a habit; habits are very hard to break, and nothing is more embarrassing than to have an adult dog attempt to 'perform' in company.

If your family consists of young active children who will teach the lively boisterous Beardie to be just as active as themselves, you will have problems unless you insist on firm handling and early training. It is sensible for just one in the family to be the trainer, feeder, and boss, so that the dog knows exactly where he stands. He could serve several masters, but it would be confusing for him.

As soon as the puppy wakes up in the morning, has a meal or drinks water, he should be put outside in the garden or yard; he will run to his favourite spot to relieve himself. If this favourite spot is right in the middle of a pretty flower bed, it is best to reorganise the garden rather than try to get him to go elsewhere; he has chosen his place, as a creature of habit and to try and persuade him to another part of the garden is likely to confuse him. As a result he might well choose the sitting room carpet. This is one of the few instances in which the dog should be allowed to have *its* way.

You should combine house training with lead and collar training. When your puppy is ten weeks old, take him into the garden and put a very light collar on him. (Make sure you have time to concentrate on this short training session.) Let him play around while wearing the collar; he will stop several times to try and scratch it off, but get him to play with his toys so that he eventually gets used to and accepts the feel of the collar. Then attach a very light lead to the collar, and let it trail on the ground as he moves around. All the time encourage him to play with a ball or other toys to take his mind off the collar and lead. Now hold the lead, but so loosely that there is no restriction on the puppy's movement. Follow him wherever he goes, all the time holding the lead. Little by little start to control him with plenty of encouragement. Make it more of a playtime rather than a training session; at the start the session should last for only a few minutes. Take off the lead and collar and next day start from the beginning again. As soon as the puppy goes along with you, increase the control so that he is walking on the lead up and down the garden. When he accepts this control without bucking or sitting and refusing to move, he can be taken out on the road for a very short walk, but *not* until he has had his full course of injections, about four months. Don't attempt to start the lead and collar training before ten weeks; give him time to settle properly in his new home first.

As soon as the puppy respects you he will be so keen to please you; since he will be a willing subject, it is *you* who will make or break him. Never on any account hit him with the lead or your hand. Your hand should always be used to pet him, your lead should only be used to be attached to his collar. He will then associate both with the fun of training in the garden or exercise which he will love. During the training of your puppy, take a biscuit with you when you go for a walk. If in a safe area, you let him off the lead he will run and play and will naturally be reluctant to return when you want him; call his name then, and offer the biscuit. He will run to you, and while he is eating the titbit, can be put back on the lead. If you have ever used your hand or the lead to punish him, he will remember, and seeing the lead and your hand at the ready will have the sense not to come near. If this ever happens, when you eventually do catch him, make a fuss of him (although you will certainly not feel like it), so that next time he will forget his play and come to the person he loves and trusts.

Make a practice of calling his name in a special tone of voice when he is to have his dinner, and when he is to go for a walk. Do not just put his dinner down at any old time; make sure he is away down the garden, and call, 'Come Jock, come'. Use a happy, friendly, welcoming tone of voice that he will get to recognise. In this way, he will soon learn to come to your calls.

I have seen so many novices bring their dogs to our kennels who never stop giving instructions to their poor animals in a monotone voice; instructions that are never obeyed.

This goes on in the same monotonous tone all the time the dog is in the room; I can only imagine that it is a repeat of what the poor dog has to put up with at home. Of course he takes absolutely no notice of the requests; they are not commands, he neither sits nor stands, nor goes to his owner until he is ready to do so. If you want your dog to sit on command, *command* him to do so in a firm voice and push his rear end down (if necessary hold it down), and make sure he sits until you allow him to break the sit. One command to sit should be enough, if you have taught him to take notice and obey you implicitly. If you give six requests for him to sit, the dog is sensible enough to take his time and wait for the last request to sit before he bothers to take notice.

I prefer to put my Beardie at the drop by gently pushing him down and saying, 'Drop'. The word 'Down' I keep for pushing him down when he jumps up for attention. I immediately bend over and pet him while he is 'down', because that is why he jumped up in the first place.

A problem that so many novices have is stopping the Beardie jumping up at visitors at the front door. (Most people go visiting in their best clothes, and resent the attentions of a large hairy dog.) Children that are brought to the house with their parents could be badly frightened by the boisterous behaviour of an uncontrolled dog; when they get to know him, they will know he is harmless, but first they need to get to know him. I have little patience with people who allow their dog to behave in this way, although obviously they want to stop it, or would not have asked advice. My advice, which causes them to look at me in amazement, is to ask if the visitors have come to see the dog or them. The visitors are there to see the people of the house, so why is the dog not shut out in the back garden? When the dog is older and better behaved, he can be allowed to welcome visitors at the door.

If the dog steals food, it may be because he has been fed at meal times from the table with titbits, or is not being fed sufficient food at his mealtimes, or, as I have heard of quite often, has been put on the table as a puppy to eat or be groomed. There is no reason why the dog should come to the table at mealtime; arrange to feed him before then, and put him out in the garden after.

We always check before we sell a puppy that one of the new owners will be at home at least part- and preferably full-time, but even when we are assured that situation will continue, there is always the possibility that circumstances may alter and both owners need to leave the puppy on his own throughout the day. They may then come home at night to make a terrific fuss of him. So long as he is given plenty of exercise, love and attention the older dog can adjust. He has previously known constant companionship, so it might take a little time and patience, especially if the owners come home at lunch time for him to be let out and fed. But I must emphasise that a full day is too long to leave an eight-week-old puppy; I would never knowingly allow any puppy to go where he will be left on his own all day.

The Beardie is bought to become one of the family; he must be trained to merge into the existing family pattern. The family should never alter their habits, arrangements, or mode of living to suit the dog.

Training for Show, and for Obedience and Working Tests are in chapter 9 (page 91).

DIET FOR PUPPIES
It is very important that the new owner receives a diet sheet from the breeder (that of the Beagold Kennels is printed at the end of the next chapter). This should have not only the list of food the puppy has been receiving, but the amount and the type for the future. Other information should be given on vitamins, the variety of food, and what should *not* be given. (White bread, chicken bones, rabbit bones, sweets, and cakes, too much potato, and titbits between meals, are all on the list of 'Don't give'.)

A puppy should be fed on a high-protein diet; sources include lean meat, fish, eggs, the casein of milk, some vegetables, some grain products. Carbohydrates give energy, but if given in excess produce too much weight. Some novice owners cut all the fat away from the meat before giving it to their pets, but that is wrong, since a dog needs a certain amount of animal fat, because it contains the vitamins A and D. If plenty of meat and milk is given to the pup, it is not really necessary to give cod-liver oil. Especially in the summer months, too much fat and oil can cause the dog to over-heat. The only time these supplements are needed is at the start of the puppies' lives, and when the bitches are pregnant. A well-planned, balanced diet alone will keep a puppy fit and well.

At about five months, when the puppy starts getting leggy, it may lose its appetite for a while, during teething. Soft milk foods, minced meat, etc., will be greatly appreciated while the young dog has a sore mouth and swollen gums. I change the diet slightly at this time and give the biscuit-meal soaked in gravy or boiling water; meat is either minced or cut finely, and fish is included in the diet. This diet need last only until the young dog has his adult teeth fully through.

ADVICE FROM BREEDER TO NOVICE OWNER

Novice owners are usually starting from scratch, and will need all the help and advice available from the breeder. Otherwise, they may ask for suggestions from another novice, with dire results. They should be encouraged to phone for help on any subject concerning the training and well-being of the puppy, *before* problems get established.

I have heard some incredible statements from novice owners. I asked one couple if they had a closed-in garden so that the puppy they intended to buy would be safely enclosed when on its own. They replied that the garden was safely closed in with a six-foot fence, except that on one side, there was no fence, just a hedge dividing off the next-door neighbour's land. Of course, they said, the puppy would be trained not to go out to the road that way! Another new owner phoned to ask me how she could stop the baby eating the dog's food and biscuits.

We (at the Beagold Kennels) always keep contact with our puppy buyers whenever possible, until they are confident that they can continue on their own. In fact we have quite often arranged a meeting in a hall, getting puppy owners together so that they can discuss their routine and training, and exchange ideas. We watch their progress, and try to iron out any problems before the gulf between owner and pet becomes too wide to be corrected.

Although we always give advice and instructions when they come to pick the puppy up at 8 weeks, we have found that the excited new owner is usually so keen to be on his way with his new purchase that most of the advice is never taken in. So the instructional session is planned for soon after they have taken the puppy home, and begun to realise there is more to owning the tiny well-behaved black and white bundle of fun when it turns into a live wire of activity with a voracious appetite for shoes, chair legs, carpets and prize plants.

We give the following information in a leaflet for new owners of our dogs:

'All puppies have been wormed at 5 weeks and again at 7 weeks, with tablets that are bought from the vet. Sometimes, a puppy will need to be wormed again at 6 months.

'Your puppy should receive all its injections before it mixes with other dogs or is taken out of the house or garden. Different vets have different ideas on the best course of prevention, so it is wise to discuss this with yours as soon as you take your puppy home. Breeders will have regular contact with their vets and know from previous experience what course to take, but new owners should take advice.

'If the puppy goes off its food or has diarrhoea, or is vomiting, etc., do not hesitate to contact the vet without delay.

'You should groom your puppy regularly at least once a week, from an early age, and teach it to stand quietly, then lie down and allow you to groom it all over. This is particularly important with long-haired dogs like Bearded Collies. As the coat develops, you should take care always to check for matted tangles behind the ears, forelegs, and under the tail. Also remember to check inside the ears when you groom, and never forget the teeth.'

These points are more fully discussed in the next chapter.

4 General Care, Grooming, Feeding

When allowed to live an active and natural life, with sensible diet and the regular companionship of its owner, the Bearded Collie keeps in good condition of both mind and body. The breed is a healthy one; under normal circumstances the only visits to the vet should be when the puppy is 12 weeks of age, and then again at 14 weeks, to receive vaccination against distemper (hard pad), infectious canine hepatitis, and leptospirosis. The certificate you receive includes a reminder to give regular booster doses to ensure continued protection.

With such a lively animal, you can readily see if he is ever off colour. He will refuse his meal, and be generally listless; his nose may be hot and dry. The infection may be just an upset tummy, either diarrhoea or constipation. If the stools are hard and of a white chalky substance and the bowel action is sluggish, the faeces are remaining too long in the large bowel where water is being absorbed out of them. A watery stool as in diarrhoea is not stopping any time in the bowel. The latter could be caused by spoiled food, worms, too much fat, or stale dog biscuits. If the trouble is over in a day or two with a change of diet, there is no need to visit the vet. Should illness continue longer, you should have the trouble checked. It may not be anything serious, but an early diagnosis of illness is very important for a quick recovery.

The following notes cover some of the more common developments and conditions, but I cannot emphasise too strongly that if you have any doubt about the condition of your dog, you should contact your vet.

ROUND WORMS
We worm our puppies at five weeks and then again at seven. These are the most common parasites, and the puppy needs to be wormed again at about six months of age. We use Coopane tablets from the vet. Most puppies have worms; some are badly infested. If we notice one in a litter not progressing as the others, the cause is usually worms; extra food with special care should be given to that one, once it has been wormed: it will soon catch up to the others.

TAPE WORMS

It is very unlikely that the pups will be pestered with any other type of worm other than round if they are kept under normal hygienic conditions. But I have heard of dogs and puppies being infected with tape worms, especially when the owner also keeps cats or rabbits. Dogs that have eaten rabbit droppings, the intermediate host, can quickly become infested, and may also pass them on to their puppies. White segments like rice are in the stool, or will be seen clinging to the hair around the anal passage. Treatment must be given by the vet.

FLEAS, LICE AND TICKS

Every effort should be made to keep your Beardie free of these external parasites. They can be picked up at a show after the dog has come into contact with others, or on the benches, or even after a country walk, especially where rabbits, hedgehogs, or cats have been present. There are numerous effective products that can be bought and used with success.

Remember also that *lice* can live in bedding and in the cracks of woodwork in the kennel; strong disinfectant, spray, or special powder should be used in the kennel, and the dog attended to before he goes back in. I have used a spray powder, which I regularly buy from my vet, called Nuvutop, and find this to be very effective when used regularly in the summer months. *Ticks* can be picked up from the fields, and especially where sheep have been. These attach themselves to the dog's skin and suck blood. They look like a wart lump; on the dog you see only a grey sack-like lump, the head buried in the skin of the dog. I have found the best way to remove them is to carefully hold a lighted cigarette to the end of the tick, after carefully parting the hair away, so that the whole tick falls away. On no account pull it out with tweezers, as this will leave the head in the skin, and a very bad sore will erupt.

TEETH

We have always given our dogs marrow bones, which they love. Dogs will spend hours chewing and exercising their jaws trying to get every scrap of meat and gristle off. We have never found that the chewing of bones upsets their digestive system, or breaks teeth, when they are comparatively young. We do not, however, give the old dogs marrow bones, as their digestive system is unable to cope with the extra quantity of calcium from the bones. At night we take the bones away, to wash, and if there is one dog slightly aggressive with others, it is put in a kennel on its own to enjoy the bone. We have found that the dogs keep their own teeth clean and strong, and need only a little attention with the special dental tartar scraper when they become relatively old. We never allow the Beardies to chew wood or stones, in case they break their teeth or get splinters in their throats. Too much soft tinned food, sweets, or other bad feeding, like excessive fat, will give the dog an unpleasant smell, especially when it encourages tartar to encrust around the teeth, pushing the gums back to cause infection and bad breath. Teeth cleaning should be as regular a chore as grooming and ear cleaning.

When the puppy is eight weeks or so, it should have an even mouth, with a full set of milk teeth. A slight overshot jaw structure at this age will usually be corrected when the dog is adult, but I would never chance keeping an undershot jaw, hoping that it will become even.

By the time the puppy is about six months he will have his permanent teeth; there should be 42 in all. By this age, the mouth should be level, or the upper jaw should fit slightly in front of the lower jaw. If a six-month-old dog has a badly overshot jaw at this age, it is very unlikely that it will correct itself, and the long canine teeth may grow and force their way into the dog's gums, giving it pain and trouble chewing.

The history of the Breed gives some indication how these mouth problems came about. The Bearded Collie has been made up from working sheepdogs; some had large heads with rounded jaws like Old English Sheepdogs; others came from the Border Collie strain, with the finer muzzles. When the cross-mating took place amongst the Beardie ancestors, together with the inherited sleek coats, fluffy profuse coats and large and fine heads came rounded top jaw and finer bottom jaw. The difficulties were manifested when these characteristics were all present in one animal. This is the reason why many puppies have their bottom canine teeth growing up into the top gums. The problem corrects itself, usually, when the adult teeth come through, but teeth should be watched closely, so that the strong milk teeth that have not been pushed out do not make the new teeth grow off course. Remaining milk teeth should be taken out by the vet, if necessary, before they can misplace the new teeth.

EARS
Check on the dog's ears every time you groom. Gently pull out the soft hair that grows inside, so that it does not mat, collect dust and dirt, and encourage infection. Check for grass seeds in the summer months; they may become embedded in the ear. Clean with a wad of cotton wool dipped in diluted peroxide, but squeeze out liquid so that the cotton wool is just damp. Never put water in the dog's ear. If you suspect that there is a grass seed or any other object in the dog's ear,

take it immediately to the vet; *never* attempt to meddle with the ears yourself other than to clean them.

ECLAMPSIA

This is a condition which may occur in bitches during whelping: they appear distressed, shiver, and ultimately go into a coma. It is caused by the bitch being drained of calcium in the blood when feeding a large litter and not receiving sufficient calcium gluconate in her diet. I have only had two bitches ever suffer from the malady. In those cases I could not believe that this was the cause, since I had fed both bitches with daily calcium tablets from the time they were mated. But, it was explained to me, tablets can pass straight through in their whole state; I should have crushed them in the food, or milk. Since then I have made sure that I give calcium in powder or liquid form, and I have never had any trouble. I try to make sure that the bitch gets a meal before she goes in to feed the puppies, especially if the puppies' combined weight is more than the bitch's. Strong, healthy puppies can soon drain a bitch, so a meal should be given four or five times a day; as most bitches feed puppies at regular intervals try to arrange that the meal is given to her so that she has a tummy-full before they 'empty' her.

UMBILICAL HERNIA

This can be noticed in both dogs and bitches; it is a small protrusion in young puppies at the usual opening of the navel. I have whelped many puppies, and find that it is the ones who have been pulled at by the bitch during parturition which develop this small bubble-like lump. When the bitch has allowed me to help, I hold the cord between the afterbirth and the puppy's navel while she pulls and eats the placenta, so that she cannot pull at the navel. I cut the cord about one-and-a-half inches from the navel; it then dries and drops off. I have not had cases of hernia in puppies so treated. If a hernia is present, as the puppy gets older the hard lump can grow quite large, when it is best to have it operated on.

MONORCHID

This is a dog with only one testicle. It was something we never heard of in our breed a few years ago. Lately I have heard of several dogs that have just one testicle descended into the scrotum, the other testicle not being palpable at all. Sometimes it happens that one testicle comes down but the other, although it can be felt, does not fully descend until the dog is over six months old. The dog is not sterile if he has one testicle, but I would not use him at stud. I have noticed in the past that one correct-size testicle descends into the scrotum at about four months of age, the other is very small and can only be felt; this, I believe, may mean that the dog has been badly alarmed at a crucial time when he was developing. It is a well-known fact that some puppies withdraw their testicles up into their body when frightened. By the age of six months, when it is ready for the show ring, there should be no question of the dog's entirety. (A dog is said to be 'entire' when it has both testicles correctly descended.) There has been talk of dogs becoming entire at the age of one year and even later; personally I would not keep a dog for stud work when I know that cryptorchidism runs strongly in the family.

CRYPTORCHID
This is a dog with no testicles. They may be hidden in the abdomen, which will cause sterility; most vets will advise that such a dog be castrated, because there is every possibility that the testicles somewhere in the body could become affected with a tumour or cancer. I have known cryptorchids to become quite vicious, but return to an even disposition after the operation.

ANAL GLANDS
Most dogs, usually those that live a natural life with a proper diet, are able to empty their glands and keep them healthy in the normal course of their lives. (Some young dogs at their first mating, around one year, will squirt out anal gland material; the smell is repulsive and unmistakable but this is not abnormal.) The anal glands are two little sacks, one each side of the anus; the secretion is normally of a watery consistency, but if it becomes more solid, and the glands hard and impacted, a visit to the vet must be made.

Grooming

Our breed needs no preparation for showing, other than the grooming required regularly: brushing, combing when needed, cleaning of teeth and ears, rubbing chalk block into the white parts to give extra glamour. The K.C. have now put a ban on the use of talcum powder. The Beardie is one of the few natural breeds; primping, scissoring, stripping or coat-parting should be for other long-coated breeds that have been altered to suit the whims of the exhibitors. Sadly, I detect the first signs of alteration to the natural look in the show rings; one or two top exhibitors are winning with Beardies that have been specially prepared, so who can blame the novices that follow the trend. If this is unchecked, the breed will become one of the many in which the chance of winning top awards is left in the hands of the owner who has capabilities to scissor and strip so professionally as to outshine his neighbour.

PRACTICAL DETAILS

While the puppy is still very young, it is best to get him used to the brush and comb even though the coat is still short; a grooming session should be a regular part of the training. The Beardie is a long-coated breed, and the time will come when grooming is not just for fun, but is a regular chore required to keep the dog's coat in good condition, and not badly matted and out of hand. Attended to regularly during half-hour sessions twice a week, the coat will be kept free of tangles and mats even during the moulting time.

We use a steel comb with rounded (not square) teeth. (If possible, the comb should have large rounded ends so that it does not hurt the dog.) To clean your dog's teeth, you can use either a dentist's tooth scraper, or a tooth brush used with a solution of Hydrogen peroxide. We use the J.D.S. shampoo; it is ideal for the Beardie coat, and does not soften it too much.

If possible, we pick a warm day to bath the dog, or else keep him in the kitchen by the fire, and do not allow him to go outside until he is completely dry. We use several large towels to rub the coat dry,

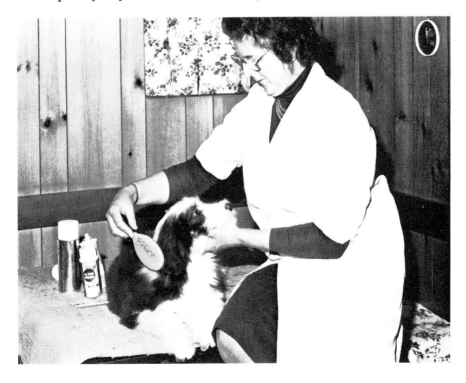

Start putting the puppy on the table for grooming at a very early age. Puppies need a lot of encouragement, and gentle but firm handling.

The puppy will enjoy grooming sessions like this one if you make them a few minutes spent regularly every week together. The puppy coat is not long to start with, so owners might be tempted to leave grooming until the coat is long and in need of grooming. This is a great mistake. Eight weeks is not too early to get the puppy used to grooming.

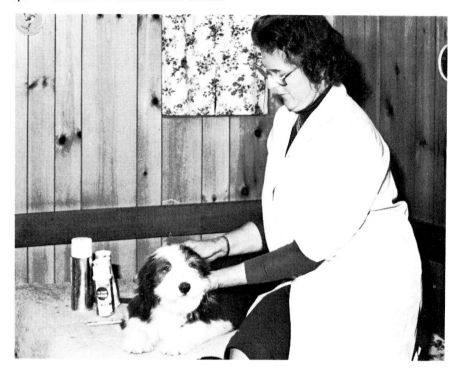

never an electric dryer. We consider that it dries the coat, causing it to break and the undercoat to come out. Even when we have used a good coat conditioner after bathing, we have found that the coat is very 'fly-away' and a moult starts if the dryer has been used. Several Beardie owners have asked me for advice on coat problems; they can usually be traced to electric dryers. Rubbing with a warm towel can be back-aching, but it stimulates the growth of the coat and the dogs like it.

As soon as the coat is completely dry, lay the dog gently on his side on the grooming table and brush this way and that way all over; brush up the legs, and from the croup towards the head; any mats or tangles should be teased out with a comb. Particular attention should be given to the parts behind the ears, under the shoulder of the forelegs, under the tail, and around the genitals. I use scissors only to clear the hair away from the penis and the area around the anus, so that a quick swab with soap and water will keep those parts clean. Wash a bitch with disinfectant, and scissor off any surplus hair that is around the vulva. Hair sometimes grows strongly in the Beardies' ears; it is best to gently pull this soft hair out so that there is no chance of it caking into a diry little mass which can harbour infection.

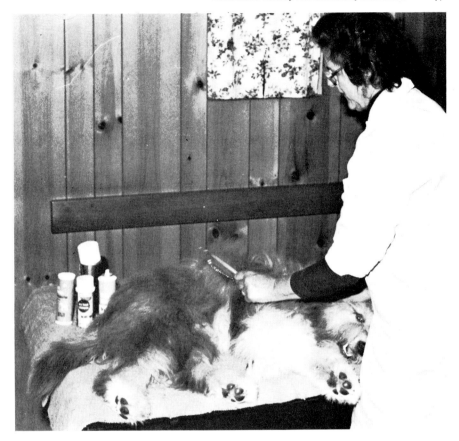

The first step in a grooming session is to get the dog settled comfortably on the table, with all the grooming paraphernalia ready for use. If necessary, he has been bathed and is now dry; a little talcum powder can be sprinkled all over one side and then brushed into the coat. Brush the coat all ways, and brush out the powder. Then do the other side. If the coat looks dry, spray it with a good coat conditioner.

The hair between the toes sometimes gets matted or muddy; but it must not be cut away, as it is a feature of the breed to have hair between the pads. First wash the feet with warm soapy water, then gently tease the tangles out. During the summer, the feet should be looked at after every walk, as there is a particularly nasty grass seed that finds its way up between the toes, under the skin, and into the pads, causing sores. The irritation makes the dog continually lick at the foot and large patches of wet eczema can result. I have even seen these grass seeds embedded in a dog's eye; Beardies, with their long coats, seem to be ideal hosts to grass seeds and thistles, so a check should always be made when they come in from their walk.

We do not cut off the dew-claws, as we consider that the working breed should be interfered with as little as possible, but we do make sure that they are kept short when we cut the nails. (Cutting is not necessary all that often, since Beardies are such active dogs that all their rushing about keeps their feet tidy.)

Hold the back foot firmly, and brush upwards. It will fall back naturally as the dog stands.

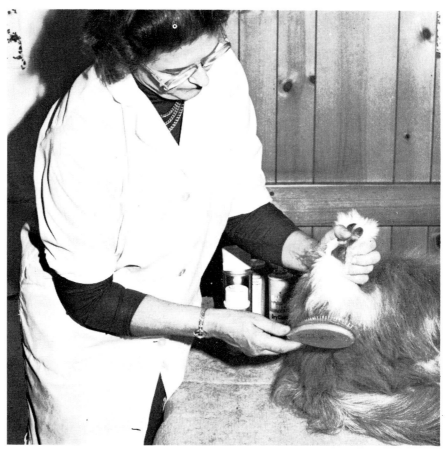

Use a steel comb to tease out tangles. Hold the tangle with your left hand close to the skin, then gently and little by little tease out the mat with down strokes, using the end of the comb. A very bad mat will take a little time, but once it is out, it will not look as if the coat had been cut, as may happen if the coat is torn by over-rough combing.

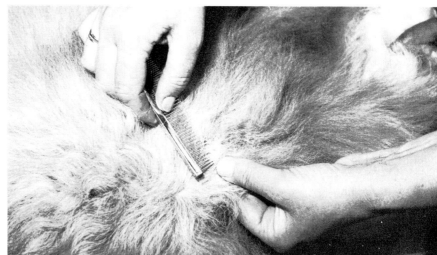

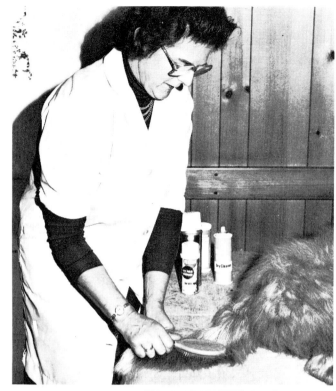

Hold the tail flat on the table and brush the fringe. Make sure that no tangles or mats are left around the genitals. I do scissor away hair from around the penis, with someone holding the dog to prevent it moving. This ensures that all that area is kept clean.

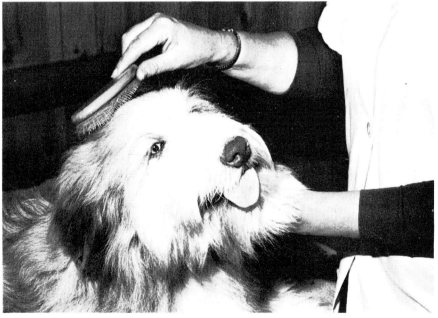

Brush all the hair back and away from the eyes. Hair on the muzzle can be brushed down to mingle with ear fringes and beard. The hair will spring naturally back in a spiky fringe over the eyes, and will be kept from obscuring the eyes by the growth of hair protecting the eyes. The beard should be brushed forward.

Preparation for shows

It should only be necessary to bath Beardies a week before a show; if they get particularly dirty, but live in the house; a bitch, when she has finished her season; or a bitch after she has had puppies. Even then, if a dog is a regular show-goer, it should not be bathed before every show.

The main grooming, bathing and preparation should be started a week before the show, so that the coat settles down again. If the weather has been particularly wet, the feet will need to be washed again the day before the show, and dusted with chalk block. (But even the journey from the car park to the bench can give the disastrous impression that the Beardie has just wallowed in a ditch full of water.) It is wisest to prepare for such an emergency by having to hand a couple of towels, chalk block, and all the grooming paraphernalia.

I have been to shows where the rain and mud have taken over, and we exhibitors have stood in wet-weather tents holding our dogs in our arms while slowly sinking into the soft muddy ground. One show provided wet-weather accommodation as big as a postage stamp; the dogs splashed up and down for the Judge to assess movement nearly in pitch darkness: the clinging wet coats showed up the good and poor outlines as never seen before. The worst show of the lot was the one which had put their wet-weather tent several hundred yards from the showground up a steep hill. The water poured down the hill in rivers as the exhibitors struggled up carrying their soaking-wet Beardies, some wrapped in towels already wetter than the dogs. I had taken three dogs to that show, and by the time I had been up and down the hill three times I was exhausted; even though I won Best of Breed with one of the dogs, I could not summon up enough energy to carry the dog up the hill again to compete in the Group.

Smooth-coated breeds present fewer problems, and their owners do not need to watch the weather quite so closely. It is quite disheartening to have a strong blustery wind blowing the Beardie coats so as to completely obliterate their shape and movement. It is miserable trying to show a Beardie under those conditions, and very difficult to judge them. So often we have spent hours preparing our dogs for the show only to have all our efforts wasted when we find that the car park is quite a long way from the show ground. We then have to wade through mud and possibly cow manure, carrying our Beardies wrapped in towels so that they arrive at the benches in a pristine state.

The Beardie coat

The Beardie coat is very short at birth, whatever colour; by the time the puppy is eight weeks of age it has grown to about an inch and a half, with a noticeable rosette around the muzzle, just covering the eyes. Ear fringes will have grown at this age, but still stick out in all directions. Even with such a short coat, it is wise to spend time every week grooming the puppy. You may see dandruff in the puppy coat, which may mean that the puppy is not getting enough fat or oil in its diet, so that the coat and skin is dry. By the time the puppy is six months old, the coat will settle down more; the colour will be strong, and the pigment should completely cover the nose and mouth. It is very difficult to generalise in the breed; some puppies have flowing coats at a very early age and never seem to moult (it is then necessary to groom regularly); others have a good coat up to about six months and then drop the lot and stay short coated right up to and sometimes over a year. If we have a puppy that is slow in growing its coat, we give extra vitamin supplements in its diet, and stop grooming weekly (we just make sure that the coat does not tangle behind the ears, etc.). Leaving the coat alone, except perhaps giving an all-over brushing once a month, the coat will grow thickly but slowly, and stay until the next change at about eighteen months.

From eighteen months onwards, the adult coat grows; it should be strong, and either straight or with a *slight* wave. Grooming can be done once a week unless the dog is always out in the mud and wet. Many coats are soft, and are rather curly on the rump even though the coat is straight on the head, shoulders and withers. A good coat conditioner sprayed into the curly parts and plenty of brushing will help keep the hair down, but as soon as the wind blows the coat about, the curls will show again. This suggests that somewhere in the ancestry of the dog was an Old English Sheepdog type.

Many Beardies have stains around their mouths. Try as you may to keep the whiskers and beard white, as soon as the dog drinks or eats the stain is back again. Some owners try always feeding dry food, but Beardies like a mixture of meat and vegetables with 'gravy', and even if they have their faces washed after each meal, by the time they have panted and 'hoovered' up the smells on their country walks, they will be just as brown stained as before.

If you allow an adult show Beardie to run with a puppy, the carefully nurtured adult coat will soon be pulled out. Puppies just love to tug at an adult's coat; I have often taken tangles of pulled-out long hair from a puppy's mouth.

When the hair is of the correct texture, if the dog shakes itself, you will see the hair on the back fall into a natural parting, and the hair on the back of the neck part naturally either side of the dog's withers. The hair on the head should arch in spiky fringes over the eyes and down over the ears. The hair on the muzzle should fall naturally each side, blending with the beard.

Feeding

This is the leaflet we give to the new puppy owners.

An eight-week-old, born-black puppy, has a short coat.

A six-month-old puppy has a coat beginning to grow into shape, and changing to grey.

Compare the two with this adult Beardie with its full coat, and being the finished product it will go back to dark grey, its colour at birth.

8 weeks to 12 weeks

'8 a.m. Breakfast	2 tablespoonfuls porridge (made not too thick), Farley's Rusks, Shredded Wheat, or any other cereal given with about a half pint of warm milk; this can be cow's, goat's, or evaporated milk. 'Stress' or any similar calcium additive should be added to the milk meal. Twice a week an egg yolk can be whipped in with the milk.
12 noon Lunch	A variety of meat will keep the dog interested in eating; minced morsels, minced meat, boneless fish, tinned Puppy Pedigree Chum, mixed with fine brown-flour biscuit meal. I always soak the biscuit meal in either hot water or gravy, then allow it to cool before adding the meat or fish. I find that puppies do not like Bisto gravy, but do appreciate Oxo or Marmite gravy. I use a handful of biscuit meal to a quarter of a pound of meat.
5 p.m. Dinner	As Lunch
10 p.m. Supper	As Breakfast

'Give yeast-based condition tablets such as Vetzyme to keep the puppy in peak condition. Some owners may prefer to give Purina dog food, a dried food with a balanced ration and complete diet. Do make sure that you add water to the meal, and that water is always available for puppies when they are fed any dry food.

12 weeks to 14 weeks

'8 a.m. Breakfast	Continue giving the puppy the same milk food for breakfast; if they will not eat their porridge, and prefer to drink the milk on its own, give it with two slices of hard-baked brown bread. Puppies love to eat rice pudding or any other milk pudding, which can be given as a 'treat'.
12 noon Lunch	The same meat meals, but increase the amount depending on the size and substance of the puppy.
7 p.m. Dinner	The meat should be increased to 1 lb a day, plus fine biscuit meal and gravy. Chopped tripe makes for variety in the diet.

14 weeks to one year

'You will notice when your puppy is needing less food or more, by the way he waits for his meals. If he is not interested, and leaves his dinner, take it up immediately and put his dish down only when he does show interest and starts looking around for food. A change of diet made now will whet his appetite again. He should be eating only three meals per day at this age, and as he gets to a year old, may be content with only two, the breakfast milk meal, and the evening meat meal.

Adults

'We find that our dogs keep in perfect health and condition with two meals a day, plus all the additives:

The main meal is: 1 lb meat, $\frac{1}{2}$ lb biscuit meal, $\frac{1}{4}$ lb 'Vitalin' (a vitamin supplement containing A, D and E), and calcium and phosphorus supplements.

Breakfast is milk and porridge, or just milk and baked brown bread.

We often give them a marrow bone to keep their teeth clean and healthy.

Fresh water should be available at all times.'

5 Kennel Management

This chapter includes a detailed description of the routine at our Beagold Kennels. Other kennels may be run on completely different lines, but whatever system is used, and however many dogs you keep, success can only be attained by sticking to a few basic rules: always feed at the same time every day; stick to a regular routine as near as possible throughout the day; clean kennels mean healthy dogs; good organisation makes less work; regular inspection of all the dogs every day keeps the vet's bills to a minimum; give extra attention to puppies and brood bitches. Your Beardie, whether he lives with others in a kennel, or in the house as a pet, needs a good mixed diet, plenty of fresh air and exercise, regular grooming, companionship, training, and lots of love and attention.

Many years ago, I started, as do so many others, with just pet dogs; I then became more ambitious, and bought a bitch to breed from. Gradually the dog population in the house increased to such an extent that the family complained: some had either to go or to be kept in kennels in the garden. My first efforts at keeping kennels was very half-hearted; the dogs spent all day in the house, but slept in the kennels. This was not a satisfactory arrangement, and I found out then that it had to be one way or the other with no half-measures. None of the dogs would settle in the kennel when he had tasted the luxury of the house; they were forever chewing or scratching the woodwork to find the exit. The only ones that lived quite happily outside were those that were born away from the house and had spent their puppy days living in kennels. I also found that giving the dogs alternate weeks in the house and out in the kennels did not work; it just made them *all* unsettled.

It was then that I formed my ideas about the best lay-out for a workable and easily manageable kennel, where the dogs gained comfort and a sense of security from having their own abode. Each dog had his own individual kennel, with chain-link partitions so that they could see each other; each could live on its own, but need not be alone. I bought small wooden sleeping-quarters, but found that the dogs were more comfortable and happier on a bench off the ground, well protected from draughts. (With the bench type of sleeping-quarters, it was easier to keep them clean, there was easier access, and it did not entail half so much bending.) In winter I used old carpets for bedding, on the benches, small pieces that could be scrubbed. (I was forever worrying friends to part with their old rugs and carpets, as the pieces soon became too dilapidated to use.) I once tried straw for the beds, but the Beardie coat was forever getting tangled with straw; newspaper was not successful either, as the print made the dogs' white parts a dirty grey. The dogs chewed up blankets to shreds. It finally had to be bare boards in the summer, carpet in the winter (and even that had to be nailed down).

PURPOSE-BUILT KENNELS
In 1970 my husband and I moved to a de-licensed public house in the country, which had much ground and many large barns ideal for conversion into kennels. Here I was able to put my ideas into practice, and eventually had built: a whelping room, puppy run and kennel; six kennels and runs for the bitches; and, in a different part of the grounds, six kennels for the dogs; with one large exercise yard.

Then working on my own, I was right to have only twelve kennels. Beardies are very active and lively, and need plenty of exericse and a daily grooming session; with all the other time-consuming jobs, I was kept busy from early morning to late at night. Several kennel girls came, and went, mostly overseas students who wished to learn and spend their holidays in England. Some young girls came who had cherished from their early school days, the idea that working with animals was a joy beyond compare. The beliefs changed when they were shown the bucket, shovel and broom that would be their daily companions to clean up manure. Some started well but gradually came to leave unmistakable lumps under clean sawdust in the exercising yard, or in the kennel. Others came to work decorated with masses of jewelry, and dressed in clothes quite unsuitable for work in kennels. I decided then that it was far less trouble and bother if I did the work myself. (One young lady told me that she did not like cleaning up manure, so she was leaving to become a kennel manageress. I explained to her that she would still be expected to clean up even as a manageress. I was a kennel *owner*, and I still had to do the menial tasks.)

So it was with great pleasure that I welcomed my long-standing friend Felix Cosme as a partner in my Kennels; I knew that he would be just as keen and interested in dogs as I was. Mr Cosme had come to England for a tour of duty with the U.S. Navy in 1967. He lived at Chinnor, and was working with the U.S.A.F. He was able to exhibit his German Shepherd Dogs in his spare time. I was then Secretary of the Hitchin and District Canine Society, and met him when he came to exhibit his dogs at the show. On his return to the States he continued both to show his own dogs and to handle for friends. He attended the U.S.A.F. Patrol-dog School, doing 'man-work', drug detection, and kennel management. In 1973 he was given a licence by

Plan of the layout of each double kennel at Mrs Collis's Beagold Kennels.

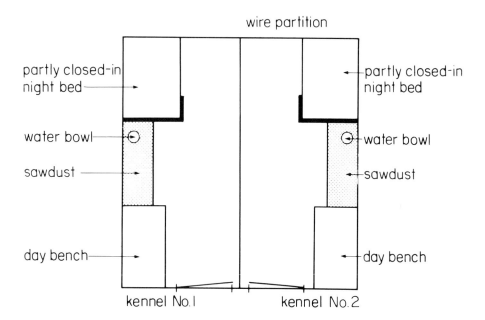

wire partition

partly closed-in night bed

water bowl

sawdust

day bench

kennel No.1

partly closed-in night bed

water bowl

sawdust

day bench

kennel No.2

the American Kennel Club to handle German Shepherd Dogs professionally. Returned to England in 1976, he spent a short time in G.S.D. Kennels; he then decided to accept a partnership in the Beagold Kennels. He considered it an interesting challenge to change to another breed, one which was similar in some respects to the G.S.D., but requiring different methods in exhibiting, handling and grooming. With the expert advice and help that he contributed, we were able to extend the kennels, and incorporate many new ideas for the comfort of the dogs and the improvement of the daily routine. We copied the system he had learnt at the U.S.A.F. School; the dogs then know what to expect and when to expect it.

Meals are served at regular times, in steel dishes for easy cleaning. Since the dogs hear the same noises from the kitchen every day, and smell the food being prepared, by the time the food is served, their salivary glands have got them drooling; every dish of food is cleared up in next to no time, and we have no fussy eaters. The older dogs are quite satisfied to have their main meal at 5.30 p.m. We now have an extra puppy kennel, so that we can separate the sexes when we take a large litter away from their mother at six weeks: this allows us to watch that none of the puppies is pushed out by bigger and stronger litter-mates. We have another bitches' kennel and run, so that a bitch is able to adjust to life away from her puppies on her own and not be worried by the other bitches. There are now eight dog kennels with their own covered-in runs. The grooming room is equipped with a carpeted bench for the dog to lie full out in comfort to be groomed; there are three small wire-fronted partitions so that the dogs can be shut away to dry, or be kept clean before a show.

The daily routine

Dogs in a house sleep peacefully until they are disturbed by the family coming down to breakfast; not so dogs kept in kennels. In both summer and winter, the birds give the dawn chorus and the dogs feel it their duty to accompany them. We give the noisiest ones an early breakfast, and hope the rest will settle down until we have had ours. At a more civilised time, around 7.30 a.m., we let all the dogs out into their runs. The brood bitches and pups are given their breakfast. Then twice a day they are taken out into the grass compounds, where they dig and play together. The dogs are sometimes boisterous but never vicious, in fact the older dogs are very gentle with the younger ones, it is the two year olds who can do damage to each other, so they are always under supervision when playing together. To make sure that harmony continues we never feed *en masse*; each dog is shut away in its own kennel to chew bones or to eat food.

After collecting the dishes used in the first meal of the day, we start kennel cleaning. We have arranged that each kennel has a low board partition with sawdust liberally strewn about in it. Dogs and bitches will change their nasty habit of messing anywhere in the kennel at night if they are given sawdust. The sawdust is shovelled up into a sack, disinfectant is put down, and then more clean sawdust. All drinking bowls are washed, and clean water provided. We keep pebbles in part of the bitch-and-puppy compound, as it improves the dogs' feet, and gets them used to all sorts of ground that they might be called to walk on.

Some of the bitches may choose to mess on the pebbles rather than on the cement compound; this is more difficult to rake up. (I remember once just before guests arrived I had gone out in the pebble compound to rake up the manure into a heap; having done so, but before I could shovel it into a sack, the guests arrived. I welcomed them then dashed out to finish my job; not noticing one of my non-doggy friends had followed me, until she said, 'Aren't your dogs marvellous doing their toilet all in one place?')

The cleaning over, we start exercising, which takes us up to lunch time. Brood bitches and puppies are again fed. Beardies are boisterous, and, if kept in kennels, chewers; most of the doors show signs of their activities, so we usually have to do some repair work as well during the day.

During the week we collect sawdust from a local sawmill, and twice a week we collect the meat from the butcher.

The kitchen
The dog kitchen has a large sink with running water, a meat safe and deep freezer. Several large plastic dustbins hold biscuit meal and complete feed; there are stacked tins of Pedigree Chum that we use sparingly in an emergency, and shelves containing vitamins (Vetzyme tablets, seaweed powder etc.). When we cook the food, we use a pressure cooker, but we feed mainly raw paunch; this has to be washed and cut, which takes quite a long time.

Whelping rooms
We have three whelping rooms, all equipped with infra-red lamps. These rooms need to be kept scrupulously clean. Keep an extra bulb as a spare for the lamps. When the puppies are first born, I tack a piece of blanket in the whelping box; as they get older and move about, I use torn up newspaper in the sleeping part and flat newspaper elsewhere. (We go through an awful lot of paper this way, but we collect it from friends, storing it up all the time for when we have puppies.)

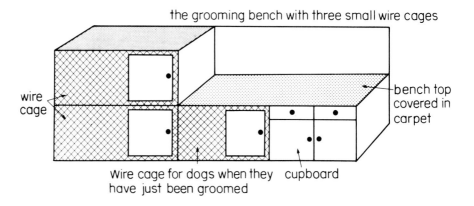

the grooming bench with three small wire cages

wire cage

bench top covered in carpet

The grooming bench used at Beagold Kennels.

Wire cage for dogs when they have just been groomed   cupboard

The grooming room
The grooming room is a real necessity for our breed of dog. We have converted quite a large room so that we can keep all the grooming paraphernalia in one place. There are three wire-fronted cages built beside and under the grooming bench, large enough for the Beardies

to move around comfortably; they can be placed there after they have been bathed and groomed, before they go to a show, or before being returned to their kennels. The bench is covered with a carpet so that the dogs can comfortably stretch out, and enjoy having their coats, ears, teeth and nails attended to.

It is important that we have had electric light fitted in most parts of the kennels, so that we can attend to any problems that arise in the dark winter nights.

6 Breeding and Rearing

DO YOU WANT TO BREED?

It is a great mistake for you to believe that your pet bitch must have a litter for her own good. I have kept maiden bitches of several breeds which have lived quite happily and healthily up to the ripe old age of twelve or thirteen. One Beagle bitch I owned had false pregnancies every time after her season; I never allowed her to have pups, but she lived until she was twelve. As soon as I saw the unmistakable signs of false pregnancy, I put a little Epsom salts into her drinking water, and stepped up her exercise; she soon got over her broody condition.

This is not always sufficient treatment for an excessively maternal bitch; if she is uncomfortable with a lot of milk, then a visit to the vet is sometimes necessary, either to have the bitch spayed, or to have injections to dry up her milk. Allowing her to have a litter will solve that problem only that time; the next time, when she is not mated, she will probably be worse. There are also many owners who think it is good for a bitch to have a litter to correct bad temperament; from personal experience I can only say that I would never attempt that remedy again. We had a 'rescued' bitch who could not settle down. We thought a litter might calm her and bring out her maternal instincts, but we had no idea of what her life had been like before we had her, or what treatment she had been subjected to by her previous owner. When her litter was born, she panicked with the pain of the birth and bit the puppies. We were able to save three, but we had to muzzle her and hold her down in order to feed them. After a few days she did accept them, but we were never able to leave her alone with them. The puppies are now grown and healthy, but the bitch was spayed.

The only permanent difference a litter will make to a bitch is to maker her look more mature. The body thickens and develops, and there is a noticeable drop in the brisket. A bitch of two years old held back in the show ring by being a slow maturer can benefit from having a litter; however, you should remember that it will be over six months before she will return to her original bloom and be in full coat.

If you have weighed the pros and cons and decided that you can cope with a litter, remember that not only must the bitch have a suitable quiet place away from noise and household traffic while she is getting used to her whelping quarters, but that she must also be allowed privacy and peace while she is whelping, and for a week or two after the puppies are born. It is not fair to have the usual comings and goings of a noisy and boisterous family interfering and upsetting the bitch, who wants to be left alone where she can rest and bring up her demanding family. Only the person who feeds her, cleans her whelping box, and exercises her will be always welcome.

WHELPING – WHERE?
Sometimes the bitch has her own ideas about where she wants to have her puppies. It is best to make sure she has them where you want her to.

It doesn't always work out as planned. One gentleman brought his bitch to be mated to one of my dogs several years back; it was the first time he had bred from a bitch, and he wanted to do it right. He phoned me every week at first, asking advice; then his secretary began to phone and take down notes. He wanted to do his best for the bitch; nothing was too much trouble. He cleared out his sauna room and converted it to a whelping room for the bitch. As the time grew near I suggested that he should shut her up in the room at night to make sure she got used to the whelping box, and the surroundings; he did not like that idea, however, replying that she had always had her freedom at night. At eight o'clock one morning shortly after, I received a telephone call; an excited but definitely upset gentleman shouted on the phone, 'What shall I do? She is having her pups on my bed!'

Choose a sheltered but open space. Under the stairs may do: it will be warm there. If they are light and airy, then a quiet tucked-away corner in the kitchen, or an outhouse (with heat if it is to be a winter litter) are good alternatives. Some provision must be made for the bitch's comfort and privacy; the area should be cordoned off so that she will feel secure from interruption. So many first-time breeders forget that the puppies will grow, from tiny little panda-like pups quite content to stay cuddled up together in the nest, to energetic, lively and very noisy bundles with the agility of monkeys and voracious appetites, long before they are ready to be sold to their new homes. Provision and accommodation must be made for them *before* whelping. (I believe that this is why so many puppies are sold before they have been completely weaned, and consequently find it harder to adjust and to cope with the upheaval of leaving their family and the warm comfort of their mother. Early separation has the effect of setting the pup back, and the change-over to a new home at a too early age usually starts with upset tummy and pitiful crying at night as soon as the pup realises he is on his own, cold, lonely, and in strange surroundings. I have found puppies are more able to cope and inquisitive enough to enjoy their new surroundings when they are eight weeks old; then, they may have one or two nights of crying, but they just need assurance from their new owners, and perhaps a warm drink of milk, and they will settle.)

Cost

With these days of high prices of dog food, high vets' bills, and the expense of Kennel Club Registrations, it is not possible both to feed the mother and her litter well, and to make any sort of profit when you sell the litter. You will be lucky if you break even.

Do consider all these factors. If you then *still* wish to breed from your bitch the suitable stud dog is the next consideration.

In-breeding

In-breeding is very close breeding within one line of animals: dogs as closely related as dog and bitch from the same litter may be bred in order to establish particular points firmly. Because characteristics are so strongly 'built in' to progeny of in-breeding, it is a technique to be used with caution. It should be used only if the original stock is perfectly sound, with no known faults in their pedigrees.

Line breeding

Line breeding is the mating of animals which are from the same line or family, but not very closely related: cousin to cousin or half-brother to half-sister is the kind of relationship involved.

Line breeding is a wiser course for a novice to take; here you will see inherited traits from both parents, and the small part of new blood brought in by the slight outcross will counteract any mistakes you make from lack of information from way back in the pedigrees. Bearded collies are still only six generations, in some cases, from working farm stock. (Pedigrees of such animals used to be stamped 'Second Class'.) Ancestors of these dogs could be carrying many faults (whites, mismarking, wild temperament etc.), as well as the new blood and typical Beardie character that was the reason for using them in the first place.

Outcrossing

Outcross breeding is the mating of unrelated partners. It can be very useful for acquiring new characteristics, but it can bring in faults that you are unaware of. Another problem I find is that it is much more difficult to pick out a good puppy for show from outcross breeding; the many different bloodlines combined produce a litter of all shapes and sizes, different-textured coats, and variety of temperaments. It seems to be just little more than luck that makes someone choose a puppy that turns out a flyer.

TIMING THE MATING

When you have contacted the owner of the dog you intend to use, inform them in good time of the date when your bitch is due in season, and then again when she does come in season so that there will be no chance of the stud dog being used excessively and not being available during the week that he should service your bitch. As soon as you notice a slight swelling of the vulva, and a bright red discharge, count from that day, but also check her daily from then on, especially if you are not sure which was the first day of her season. The bright red blood discharge will change in colour to a thicker, paler discharge, also her vulva will be very soft and swollen when she is ready for mating. A bitch is usually ready to be mated from the eleventh or twelfth to the fourteenth day as the chart below advises. But we have found some bitches have short seasons, and have to be mated on the seventh or eighth day to produce puppies. On the other hand many may not accept the attentions of the dog until the twentieth day. The chart can only be a guideline to be used on most bitches. Your bitch should come into season around the age of six to

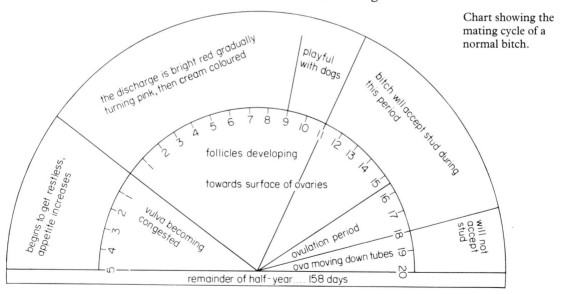

Chart showing the mating cycle of a normal bitch.

nine months, then every six months after that. Some bitches come into season for the first time at the age of one year. It is wise, if you have intentions of eventually mating your bitch, to watch her closely throughout her seasons, to count the days and check her for colour and swelling, so that when you do decide to mate her you will have some idea of what has been the previous pattern. There is no reason why she should vary from season to season. The best way to test whether she is ready to accept the dog is to gently rub your hand along the bitch's back. Speak to her, and stroke her on her hips, and then down the length of her back again. If she gets excited and arches her tail in a noticeable curve, then puts her tail to one side, you can take it that she is then ready to be mated, and should be taken to the stud dog.

Leave the owner of the stud dog to attend to the mating unless you are asked to give assistance; you may be asked to hold your bitch's head (if she is a maiden bitch she will need the comfort of someone she loves). Some bitches play up and need very firm handling; it is not always those you would expect. One bitch I took to be mated was strong-willed and difficult, and I imagined there would be difficulties; she took one look at the dog and started the courting ritual herself. Others have allowed all the advances, and then screamed as soon as the dog mounted.

This latter happening is very upsetting to some stud dogs (especially young ones), and they could be made reluctant to mount a bitch again. It is much wiser to use a proved stud dog with a maiden bitch, so that he is not put off by anything (this is another reason why I do not advocate using the pet dog from down the street).

Mrs Glynis Chambers asked us to help with a mating between her stud dog Beagold Fortune Beck and a troublesome bitch. He was not taking his work seriously at all, as we found when we arrived. Their garden backs on to the railway line, and just as Fortune Beck was about to tie a train was heard in the distance. Immediately he jumped off the bitch's back, dashed down the garden, jumped over the rockery and chased the train the width of the garden, then just as quickly dashed back, mounted the bitch and tied. Even with this casual approach the result was five beautiful puppies.

Mating is a very chancy business; so many think that if dog and bitch are allowed to run together in a garden or in a shed, the mating is a certain thing. How wrong they are! I have had many bitches brought to my dogs after some untrained dog has worried them for hours. I sometimes allow my dog to mate, but I am rarely happy about such a situation. It is quite a usual practice to ask for two matings to take place within 48 hours, as the bitch could have missed at the first mating and will conceive from the second service.

THE BITCH AFTER MATING

For the first four weeks after she has been mated, I do not treat the bitch any differently from before. She still has milk and cereal in the morning and a meat and biscuit meal in the evening. From five weeks onwards, she gets an extra lunchtime meal; extra meat or eggs, yeast tablets, vitamins A and D, and calcium. After that, I increase the meals in size only if she wants more. I cut down on long walks, and try to discourage her from jumping and rough playing (that can be quite some effort when you are restricting a Bearded Collie).

As whelping time draws near, the bitch grows quite considerably in size; her nipples enlarge, and she 'slows down' quite a bit. She will make nests around the garden or in her whelping box, where she spends time scratching up the paper, and panting.

Usually the date of whelping is between 57 and 64 days after the first mating. Some bitches, usually maiden ones, have their puppies

Served Jan.	Whelps March	Served Feb.	Whelps April	Served March	Whelps May	Served April	Whelps June	Served May	Whelps July	Served June	Whelps Aug.	Served July	Whelps Sept.	Served Aug.	Whelps Oct.	Served Sept.	Whelps Nov.	Served Oct.	Whelps Dec.	Served Nov.	Whelps Jan.	Served Dec.	Whelps Feb.
1	5	1	5	1	3	1	3	1	3	1	3	1	2	1	3	1	3	1	3	1	3	1	2
2	6	2	6	2	4	2	4	2	4	2	4	2	3	2	4	2	4	2	4	2	4	2	3
3	7	3	7	3	5	3	5	3	5	3	5	3	4	3	5	3	5	3	5	3	5	3	4
4	8	4	8	4	6	4	6	4	6	4	6	4	5	4	6	4	6	4	6	4	6	4	5
5	9	5	9	5	7	5	7	5	7	5	7	5	6	5	7	5	7	5	7	5	7	5	6
6	10	6	10	6	8	6	8	6	8	6	8	6	7	6	8	6	8	6	8	6	8	6	7
7	11	7	11	7	9	7	9	7	9	7	9	7	8	7	9	7	9	7	9	7	9	7	8
8	12	8	12	8	10	8	10	8	10	8	10	8	9	8	10	8	10	8	10	8	10	8	9
9	13	9	13	9	11	9	11	9	11	9	11	9	10	9	11	9	11	9	11	9	11	9	10
10	14	10	14	10	12	10	12	10	12	10	12	10	11	10	12	10	12	10	12	10	12	10	11
11	15	11	15	11	13	11	13	11	13	11	13	11	12	11	13	11	13	11	13	11	13	11	12
12	16	12	16	12	14	12	14	12	14	12	14	12	13	12	14	12	14	12	14	12	14	12	13
13	17	13	17	13	15	13	15	13	15	13	15	13	14	13	15	13	15	13	15	13	15	13	14
14	18	14	18	14	16	14	16	14	16	14	16	14	15	14	16	14	16	14	16	14	16	14	15
15	19	15	19	15	17	15	17	15	17	15	17	15	16	15	17	15	17	15	17	15	17	15	16
16	20	16	20	16	18	16	18	16	18	16	18	16	17	16	18	16	18	16	18	16	18	16	17
17	21	17	21	17	19	17	19	17	19	17	19	17	18	17	19	17	19	17	19	17	19	17	18
18	22	18	22	18	20	18	20	18	20	18	20	18	19	18	20	18	20	18	20	18	20	18	19
19	23	19	23	19	21	19	21	19	21	19	21	19	20	19	21	19	21	19	21	19	21	19	20
20	24	20	24	20	22	20	22	20	22	20	22	20	21	20	22	20	22	20	22	20	22	20	21
21	25	21	25	21	23	21	23	21	23	21	23	21	22	21	23	21	23	21	23	21	23	21	22
22	26	22	26	22	24	22	24	22	24	22	24	22	23	22	24	22	24	22	24	22	24	22	23
23	27	23	27	23	25	23	25	23	25	23	25	23	24	23	25	23	25	23	25	23	25	23	24
24	28	24	28	24	26	24	26	24	26	24	26	24	25	24	26	24	26	24	26	24	26	24	25
25	29	25	29	25	27	25	27	25	27	25	27	25	26	25	27	25	27	25	27	25	27	25	26
26	30	26	30	26	28	26	28	26	28	26	28	26	27	26	28	26	28	26	28	26	28	26	27
27	31	27	1	27	29	27	29	27	29	27	29	27	28	27	29	27	29	27	29	27	29	27	28
28	1	28	2	28	30	28	30	28	30	28	30	28	29	28	30	28	30	28	30	28	30	28	1
29	2			29	31	29	1	29	31	29	31	29	30	29	31	29	1	29	31	29	31	29	2
30	3			30	1	30	2	30	1	30	1	30	1	30	1	30	2	30	1	30	1	30	3
31	4			31	2			31	2			31	2	31	2			31	2			31	4

Table showing when a bitch is due to whelp.

early, especially if it is to be a large litter; others may have them one
or two days late. It is not unusual for a bitch carrying only one or
two puppies to go four days late. We bring our bitches into the
whelping room about a week before they are due to whelp, to accustom them to their new surroundings and to let them arrange the
bedding as they want it in the whelping box. The bedding can be
sheets of torn-up newspaper, or a tacked-down blanket, with torn-up
newspaper for her to make a nest.

It is then that we start watching constantly; if the bitch has
'dropped' and is carrying her puppies low, and is panting and unsettled, we know that her time is near. She may refuse her meals a
couple of days, although some bitches eat right up to the last, then
sick it up when their time draws near. She will relieve herself more
often than she normally does; usually this indicates that she will whelp
within a few hours, or less. Go with her into the garden, watch her,
then bring her back.

WHELPING

Maiden bitches sometimes panic; with the more painful contractions
they may scream and try to reach round to their rear. Hold them
firmly in such cases, and try to calm them down. Even if the first
puppy causes panic during labour, once the bag emerges, the natural
instinct usually overcomes fright; after the birth the bitch herself will
attend to cleaning up the puppy. While she is eating the afterbirth
and licking herself clean, I take the opportunity to rub the puppy dry
in a warm towel.

Sometimes the puppy's first cry sounds a bit 'watery', but its mouth
and throat soon clear, and the pup will search for its first meal.

If the cord which has joined the puppy to the placenta has been
bitten off by the mother closer to the puppy than it should have been
(an inch to an inch and a half is correct), I put a dab of iodine on the
end of the cord to seal its bleeding. The iodine will also make the
bitch leave that part of the pup alone; constant licking by her might
start the cord bleeding again. In an hour it will be sealed and dry.
From then on we work together until I am sure the last puppy has
arrived, I offer her a drink of glucose and milk, which she greedily
accepts throughout the whelping. If it is a long tiring whelping, with
sometimes an hour's lapse between the birth of each pup, and more
than six puppies born, a bitch will drink a couple of pints of milk,
with a teaspoon of glucose (no more) to each pint. We have had
bitches go three hours between each pup, which is a long time - but
if she is not unduly disturbed, and the contractions not very painful,
we allow natural whelping without calling in the vet. She will not
finally settle until the last pup has arrived. Some bitches will be

persuaded to go outside to relieve themselves, but not very often will a bitch leave the pups that have already been born.

When it is all over, I change her bedding, and settle her down to sleep and suckle her new infants. I make sure that all are sucking lustily. If there is a litter of eight or less, there is a teat for each pup, and no problem. A difficulty arises when there are more, and there is then extra work to see that the puppies are fed in rotation. The bitch's milk has to be supplemented, with extra feeds for the smallest ones twice a day. It is noticeable that the largest puppies empty a teat then move to the next one, usually pushing away a smaller and weaker puppy who needs help to hold on. The only way to be sure that all are receiving the same amount of food is to lift up each puppy after a meal, or three or four times a day and feel that they are full and rounded like their brothers and sisters. You can soon tell if one is being pushed out and not getting a fair share. We are never without a Catac Foster Major Feeding Bottle, and a tin of Lactol, in case we have to supplement the bitch's milk, for a weakling, or for an extra large litter. The instructions for use are sold with the bottle, together with six different sizes of teats.

After Whelping

The first three days are the most critical. We watch the puppies constantly for any signs of trouble, as it would be heartbreaking to lose a puppy at this stage. So long as the bitch settles and eats well, and the puppies suckle contentedly, they will thrive. We feed the bitch on milk, cereals and white fish only for the first three days. The amount she will eat varies, but some food is left down for her all the time. Some will eat tripe as well; others may refuse everything but liquids. Then return to the normal diet, plus extra milk, scrambled egg, and as much red meat, either cooked or raw, as is needed to keep her interested in food at all times. Seeing the contented mother nursing fat whelps under a warm light in a spotless kennel is a rewarding sight, and gives one a feeling of achievement.

We expect each member of an average litter of seven to weigh from 12 to 16 oz at birth. At one week old, the puppies should each weigh between 1 lb 6 oz and 1 lb 8 oz. They should then continue to gain weight evenly, until they weigh about 3 lb 8 oz at three weeks. Their eyes start to open at ten days, and open fully by the twelfth day.

At three weeks you should be able to feel tiny sharp teeth pricking through their gums in the front of their mouth. At the back, the double teeth take longer to come through, and you can feel large skin-covered lumps in their jaw at five or six weeks.

If the litter is large, we start to wean the pups at three weeks, giving them little balls of scraped lean raw meat. They usually need little persuasion to eat and, soon getting the idea, will suck madly till the meat is all vacuumed in. Feeding is easier if you have a partitioned kennel; otherwise you may find yourself feeding the same pup twice. This is not disastrous when feeding: it is when you worm the pups or give medicine that it is imperative to know which ones have been dosed, and which ones have not.

Filabey Heinkje
with eight puppies
four days old.

All the handling, petting and other attention the pups get at this stage is the first contact they have with humans. It is so important to gain their confidence and 'make a good impression'. We start calling them by name, and talk to them whilst feeding them. This accustoms them to the human voice; soon if you call 'Come pups' at feeding time, they will appear from everywhere and scamper to see what you have to offer. This is the beginning of training them to come immediately they are called.

Before long, the pups will be eating three solid meals a day, and the bitch will be visiting them only at night to feed them the fourth meal. We deliberately give a variety of food so that when the pups go to their new homes they can cope with any food they may get.

Mrs Irene Kiff's Elsmlow Maid Megan at Fenacre; fawn bitch with puppies sired by Ch. Edenborough Star Turn at Beagold.

Breakfast usually consists of three cakes of Weetabix, a tablespoon-ful of Farex with one pint of milk, for six five-week-old puppies. The equivalent amount with porridge, or any other cereal. Lunch is cooked minced meat, or tripe, or fish added to fine brown biscuit-meal that has been soaked in meat gravy, allowing about three table-spoonfuls for each puppy of this mixture. The 6 p.m. feed is the same; at this age we give more meat and only a little added biscuit meal. We also add the vitamins with Stress, Vetzyme, and a sprinkling of Vitalin on the food. Even though the bitch might feed the pups at night we also feed them at 10 p.m. with a milk meal the same as breakfast.

The pups should be wormed at 5 weeks and again at 7 weeks of age with the tablets from the vet.

The whelping box (or kennel) has three compartments. First, a partition is put up so that the bitch is under the warm lamp with her pups tucked nicely close to her, with just enough room so that she can come and go without having to tread on the litter, but not so much room so that a pup can roll away from her warmth. At about three weeks of age the pups are able to totter away from the nest to urinate, so we take down the first partition for them to mess on paper away from where they sleep. Each pup in turn, as it wakes up, goes as far away from the nest as it can to mess, so keeping the nest clean. The third partition is high enough for the bitch to see her pups but also to be on her own, and keep away from the constant demands they make on her milk. Whenever we bring the pups in to play with them in the kitchen we put down paper, and they will walk the length of the kitchen to use it.

Having been trained to mess on newspaper, with worming completed, and eating with a healthy appetite, our puppies can adjust to their new homes at eight weeks of age.

Meanwhile, the bitch has usually tired of motherhood, and returns to her own kennel quite contented. Her milk will have dried up by this time, but from five weeks onwards she will regurgitate food she has eaten whenever she visits the pups; they do not need this food, as they are already full from their own meal, and she needs to build up her strength again. Most bitches regurgitate and leave the soft food for the puppies to eat; some regurgitate then growl warningly at the puppies and eat the food again themselves. Some bitches can be very rough with the puppies when they play, especially if the pups start nuzzling for milk and the bitch cannot get away. So although play looks very touching for a while, I do not allow it to last for long, and I listen for yelps as her heavy paw descends on a tiny body, or a sharp nip sends a pup scurrying for shelter.

THE BITCH AND WHELPING

I am always very surprised when I see bitches being shown in full coat when they have had a litter only ten weeks before, but some bitches do remain in sufficiently good condition. I do not know why some lose their coat completely whilst others retain it. Our bitches seem to give all their attention and nourishment to their pups, and debilitate themselves to such an extent that they lose what little coat they have left. I also cut away the long hair around the teats and back passage of the bitch before she whelps. I learnt my lesson when one bitch I owned changed, for no reason that I could understand, from being a good mother to growling at her four-week-old pups. I checked her, and found that the hair had wound around one of her nipples; the puppies' sucking had tightened the hair so much that it had cut into the nipple badly, and it was giving her pain. I carefully cut the hair, washed the very sore part, then supervised the feeding, to make sure that no pup sucked at that teat until it had healed. Another reason for cutting back the long hair is to prevent pups getting tangled in the coat: I once had a shock when a bitch came out of her whelping box to greet me with a puppy tangled in her beard under her chin! I soon got out the scissors and trimmed her beard short. What coat is left is often pulled out by the tiny puppies scrambling over her; the poor ragged-looking bitch then usually starts a big moult, only growing back into full coat about six months later.

I aim to mate my bitch for the first time at between eighteen months and two years. If a bitch has had only two or three pups, I do not think it harms her at all to be mated again at her next season, providing that starts from nine months to a year later, and she is in tip-top condition. She must then be rested for two years. The snag is that bitches rarely come into season regularly, although there are those that have a season every six months, and then a breeding programme can be planned and timed for the summer litter. When a lot of bitches live together, it is quite usual for all of them to come into season at the same time; difficulties arise when you have facilities for two litters only. The number of litters a bitch can have throughout her lifetime depends on her health, the facilities available, and how often she comes into season. No definite plans can ever be made.

Our printed stud cards, apart from the pedigree of the dog which is to sire a litter, state that no bitch will be accepted for mating at our Kennels after they have reached the age of seven years. We feel that when a bitch reaches the veteran stage she should be allowed to rest on her past glories.

7 The Stud Dog and Mating

A terrific lot of thought should go into your planning before you choose a stud dog for your bitch. It should be your aim to produce puppies better than their parents whenever possible. Studying pedigrees is one of the ways to start so long as you can see from the pedigree of your bitch what the experienced breeder had in mind to establish a good line. Studying the Championship Show wins of a dog is not always a good guide: the dog you see in front of you might not produce his like; he might be just one in the litter that has turned out to be a high flyer. So using him could well produce a mixture of types with nothing at all like the sire. We have based our breeding on two good strong lines; with our own bitches of similar breeding and type we now can tell from each litter what to expect. By careful breeding we do not need to go outside for stud dogs, but keep four mainly of the lines that will tie in well with our bitches.

We do receive enquiries from bitch owners asking what colour dogs we have at stud, illustrating that that seems to be the main criterion with so many would-be breeders. They either want a dog that does not sire brown puppies, or they want one that sires mixed colours, while others are very keen to produce blue puppies. They seem to forget that the colour combination comes from the dog *and* the bitch, and if these colours are not in the pedigree it is very unlikely that they will get what they hope for.

We take it for granted that the prospective breeder has studied the pedigrees of both dog and bitch so that there will be a litter showing all the necessary requirements. When we are shown the bitch's pedigree, we study the suitability of the bitch for mating, and where her owner has not decided on which stud dog to use, we will then assess the combination of the bitch with any of our dogs before advising which one would tie in well with that bitch.

To run a successful stud service in Beardies, it is advisable then to have dogs of all four colours at stud - blue, brown, fawn and black, then whatever a particular bitch's owner prefers they cannot argue about colour. With the choice of colour made, we then consider all the other necessary requirements and characteristics needed to produce good quality puppies. We also consider temperament, such an important point, as this is certainly passed on to the progeny. So long as the visiting bitch is of good sound temperament, healthy, and does not have the same faults that the dog of the owner's choice has, we allow the dog to mate her. We allow for nervousness on her first encounter with the dog, but do not accept excessively nervous bitches with fear in their eyes. Some owners arrive with a definite preference for one particular dog, but even then it is wise to discuss pedigrees as well as the physical attributes of both, making sure that they complement each other, rather than leaving it to chance and risking mediocre puppies. A tightly curled tail in either parent could be inherited by several in the litter; poor coats (soft and curly, or very sparse with no undercoat) can also be transmitted from the parents. Of course good points are passed down as well; if your bitch excels in coat, head, temperament and shape, and the dog does also, then you have a chance of producing top quality puppies–puppies that you will be proud of either when you are showing them or just as pets.

We start a young dog at stud when he is eleven months or a year old. He is introduced to a quiet bitch, who will encourage and play with him, and when ready, will stand for him to mount her. We always hold the bitch, even when we can see that the young dog can manage on his own; we guide and help him so that when he does get a difficult bitch, he will accept help and will be willing to mate when people are around helping and watching. Some dogs do not like humans in the vicinity when mating, and will stop immediately and not continue until they are completely on their own.

When the bitch is ready, she will lift her tail to one side. The dog will mount several times, probably, before finally mating; when he does so, his penis erects inside the bitch's vagina, and a circle of muscles within the bitch then tightens to hold the two animals together: this is termed the 'tie'. The dog's forelegs may go both to one side of the bitch, and he may lift one hind leg over her back and turn to face completely in the opposite direction while they remain tied.

It is a little frightening for an inexperienced dog who has never been tied to find himself unable to move away during the mating. He may panic, so gentle words and firm handling are necessary to calm him down and reassure him that his uncomfortable posture is quite natural. Dogs are creatures of habit, and what happens at the first mating will be remembered for the next time; an enjoyable experience will be the start of a successful stud career for a keen youngster.

An experienced stud dog will know what to do. Even if the bitch is difficult and struggles, he will hold on until he has penetrated her (this moment may be momentarily painful for a maiden bitch and she might give a sharp cry). He will stay on her for a short time, until he is ready to get off her back and stand in a more comfortable position.

If necessary, he can be helped to move into the tie position by lifting his foreleg over the bitch's back and his hind leg over the hindquarters of the bitch.

The reproductive systems of a dog and bitch.

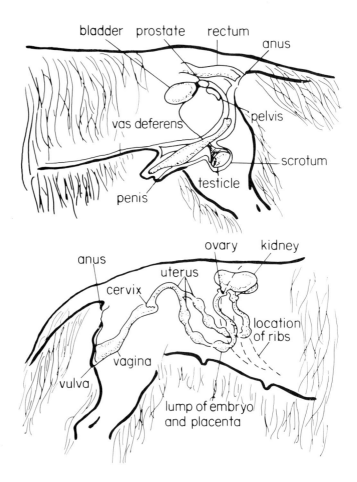

We always hold the dog and bitch while they are tied, so that there is no chance for the bitch or dog to be 'pulled around' (with the danger of internal damage), or attacked by each other. The tie can last any time from five to thirty minutes. When the bitch releases the dog, he will immediately lick himself clean; we also wipe his genitals with disinfectant. He is then returned to his kennel to rest. Do not allow him to mix with any of the other stud dogs after the mating; the scent of the bitch in season, and of the mating itself, could cause a jealous battle.

After the completion of the tie, when the dog and bitch have parted, the bitch sometimes has a blood-coloured discharge, of greater quantity than she otherwise loses in her season. This is nothing to worry about.

It may seem surprising that so much human help is given to mating dogs, but it takes time for natural matings; left on their own, dog and bitch would eventually mate, but might take three or four days over it if the bitch is maiden. For a maiden bitch, unlike a brood bitch, mating can be a traumatic experience, and she may react by snapping and fighting to get away from the dog, even before he mounts. This is so out of character for some bitches that their owners cannot believe that the bitch is not being hurt, even when they are assured that nervousness of the unknown may naturally make the bitch show wild reactions. Novice owners are also surprised that their bitch does not accept the advances of the dog immediately. They will have been advised to bring her on the 11th or 12th day when she will be ovulating; it should be an instant love match! But remember that in the wild state, the bitch is courted by numerous dogs for days, and by the time she is ready to accept the dog of her choice, she has been sexually excited and accepts the strongest dog who has fought off all his opponents.

There are always breeders who say that they prefer a natural mating, and who will mate the bitch only when and if she is willing; but this can seldom be achieved, as the owner of the bitch keen to have her bitch successfully mated must usually come to a trained stud dog. The meeting takes place, usually, after a long car journey; there is not enough time for a courtship to take place to give the dog the necessary encouragement, so second-best arrangements have to be made.

Stud dogs must be kept in tip-top condition; keeping them in a happy, healthy frame of mind is impossible if they are run constantly with the bitches. They would certainly suffer every time a bitch came into season, if they were unable eventually to mate: the mating instinct cannot be suppressed by any training. Dogs should be kept as completely away from the bitches as possible, since the scent of a bitch in season can be easily detected by dogs; even if they are simply exercised on the same ground, the discharge and urine smell would give the game away. Knowing that a nearby bitch was ready and being unable to get to her to mate her will certainly cause a dog to fret and howl, and even to lose his appetite – with the resulting loss of condition and coat. We have to be very careful to ensure that our stud dogs do not know that a bitch has been brought in for mating; we follow a strict routine of spraying disinfectant all over the dog before he is returned to his kennel, too, as the others would smell him and get the whole story.

We feed top-quality food – plenty of it – to the stud dogs, with added vitamin supplements. Correct feeding, high in protein value, is needed to keep both dog and bitch in good condition for breeding. We never accept a bitch for mating if she is over seven years of age, or the slightest bit off-colour.

We are sometimes asked why a dog is reluctant to mate a bitch brought to him. There can be many reasons, but the most frequent is that an owner has allowed the dog to be with the bitch very early in her season; a bitch will fight off any advances until she is ready, and if this goes on too long the dog will lose interest before the time the bitch is ready. Or if an owner has a dog and bitch living together, the dog will mount the bitch in play. If he is constantly chastised for doing so, he will get to the point when he stops mounting, in play or seriously. Some dogs who are advertised at stud are so humanised by loving owners that they do not have the slightest inclination to do stud work. (We always advise a one-pet dog owner to keep the dog from being used at stud; what he does not know about he will not miss. Further, a pet dog, once used, will be off searching for mongrel bitches on his own; any bitch in season within miles of his home will attract him. For the sake of the one experience, the home-loving pet dog is changed for all time. He could also revert to his natural instinct of lifting his leg in the house to mark his territory.)

Some novices who own one or two bitches decide to buy in their own stud dog, who is allowed to run with the bitches; he will attempt to mount them. If he is not to be allowed to mate, the owner must be constantly alert to see that the dog is taken away before he worries himself and the bitches throughout the whole three weeks of a bitch's season. If I am asked, I always suggest that mixing the sexes is disastrous, especially if the animals are house-pets. Bearded Collies are not aggressive or troublesome when living under normal conditions: two dogs live together quite happily. Introduce a bitch, however, and the trouble starts.

The owner of the stud dog has certain responsibilities: a dog should not be advertised at stud if it is known that he has missed to several bitches; if the dog has been allowed to mate too many bitches in a very short time, his sexual powers could easily be diminished, and the owner of the visiting bitch might wait in vain for the expected litter. A shy or reluctant stud dog should be first used on a quiet tractable bitch to encourage him to be more impetuous, and not to be put off by a token show of resistance. It is impossible to predict how a bitch will react. Even the quietest may show aggression; if the dog is easily put off by a first snap, it is unwise for an owner to advertise him as at public stud until he is completely sure that the dog will accept all comers.

We prefer not to keep the bitch for over-night boarding until after she is mated: we always feel that the bitch (especially if a maiden) will be upset enough by the experience of being mated in surroundings that are completely unfamiliar, without the added confusion of spending two or three days away from her owners and her home.

The stud fee should be paid at the time of first mating, provided there is a tie; any suggestion of a second mating, to make sure, should be left for the stud dog owner to make. If the stud dog is not in constant use, there is no reason why he should not be just as keen the next day. The stud fee should be the same price as one puppy; many owners price their dogs' worth too low, never taking into account the cost of keeping a stud dog in the tip-top condition needed for regular stud work.

We have had so many good stud dogs, but none to touch the prowess of Ch. Davealex Royle Baron. Even now, at 15 years of age, he senses when bitches are in season, although he has not sired a litter for over three years. In 1974 his reputation was well known, and I wrote an article for the *Beardie News* describing his stud career as 'zealous, eager and ardent'. I had letters from Beardie owners who had enjoyed the article, and consequently Baron's stud service was in even more demand. Baron was never trained for stud work; he found his first bitch before he was a year old, and although I have never kept a proper record of his offspring I am sure that the number must be well over three hundred now. The following passage from the article will give some idea of his keenness.

His characteristic entrance into the mating room is faster than the rocket leaving for the moon, the poor bitches never know what has hit them. No preliminary courtship from him, no check to see if she smells nice, or is in fact in season; he launches himself, ties, turns and settles down to wait deceptively patiently for his freedom, with the hope that I will be taken off my guard so that he can immediately grab the bitch and start all over again.

It is really amusing to see him walk through the bitches' kennels sniffing the air like a rutting stag as he passes by, mentally making notes and pinning his hopes on the future. Usually he is a gentleman with my own bitches; it is with the others that he tries to show his love and affection; sons, daughters, brothers, sisters, he tries to love, and he even tries to embrace his father. His mother he has not encountered for several years, but would no doubt show his affection for her in the same way.

He is what is called a 'Keen Stud Dog', especially as he checks for bitches in season in the Open Dog classes at shows.

8 Coat Colour and Pigmentation

I doubt that there is any other breed of dog which has such a wide variety of colours and shades in coat colour as the Beardie. The situation is complicated by the fact that coat colour changes as the dogs grow older.

I know of no book which covers the subject in detail; it is only from the experience of breeding so many litters from so many colour lines in the breed that I can write here with any authority.

In the section which follows, 'colour' refers to coat colour; 'pigmentation' is the colouring of skin, eye rims, nose, lips, etc.

The colour in the old Bothkennar dogs was excellent, the slates were dark with good pigmentation, the browns were as near chocolate as possible with no lack of brown pigment, but indiscriminate colour breeding has since taken place, although, Mrs Willison had always advocated breeding back to dark-slate or black for the browns and blues.

I have always been absorbed in the study of colour breeding in dogs, and I was delighted to find, when my partner Felix Cosme joined these Kennels, that he had given the same subject years of research while breeding and training German Shepherd dogs. We were able to exchange ideas, and to set about further breeding to enrich pigmentation and coat colour, whilst retaining the good qualities already established in the lines.

Certainly, looking at a show line-up of Bearded Collies, one can hardly believe sometimes that they are all the same breed, and when one ponders on the colour at birth of some of the dogs, it is not hard to realise that there is quite a mixture of blood lines from the original working sheepdogs.

Born-black puppies that will turn to silver
The colour of puppy that will change most is black. A born-black puppy from a silver grey sire and a born-brown dam (especially if back in the pedigree were several blues and browns) may be born with excellent pigmentation – black eye-rims, black nose and lips, and good white collie markings, white blaze and collar, four white paws,

and white tail tip. At about six weeks of age, shaded grey will appear on the hocks, around the eyes (like spectacles), and on the front legs; this is a good indication that the puppy will become either a very light silver-grey, or a simple grey when it is an adult. When the puppy shades to light silver-grey, uneven white markings need not cause great concern. The white will blend in with the silver coat, and much of the white collie markings will be indistinguishable. If the eyes look light in colour while the puppy is young, they will blend with the adult dog's colouring, and so satisfy the Standard's requirement, 'eye to blend with coat colour'. Another strong indication that the dog will stay pale silver is a light grey colour on the ears; if ears are lighter or darker than the main body of the coat, changes will still take place, until the Beardie reaches the age of seven or eight years, when coat colour will finally settle. The pale silver coat is very attractive, but this colour Beardie can often be seen without mouth pigment, and even pink patches on the eye rims, which is not desirable.

Born-brown puppies from blue and brown parents
I have never done this colour mating, so I can only describe what I have observed. It seems that this is another breeding combination that can produce lack of pigmentation when the dog reaches two years of age, especially if brown and blue ancestors are a large part of the pedigrees. So many born-browns change to a colour even paler than a born-fawn when they are from one blue parent and one brown. Pink eye-rims, mouth and nose show through the fast fading brown top skin; sometimes pigment returns for a little while, but usually by the time the dog is over five, pigment has gone forever. There are of course Beardies born from these colours that do retain pigment and coat colour, but the problem will usually appear somewhere in the litter. The sad thing about it is that if a bitch from the litter is mated to a similarly bred dog, the innocent buyers of the resulting litter will be confronted with insoluble problems. It is to be regretted that few breeders put the birth colours in their pedigrees.

Many breeders fall down by believing that colour can be improved by just one dark parent being introduced; in practice, colour can be corrected only by several matings to dark-pigmented dogs. Remember too that fawn is a dilution of brown, and blue is a dilution of black; even if the pale colours do look more glamorous, and are very popular in the show ring, they should be bred for gradually: never lose sight of the fact that the aim is for a light-silver coat colour with a dark-pigmented nose etc. in the finished product. Novices attempting a colour mating will look at the resulting litter of black, brown, fawn and blue puppies lying there in the whelping box, and scorn any suggestion that there could later be pigmentation problems; the problems will not even have shown by the time the litter is old enough to be sold, unless one or two do not have their noses completetely covered with colour.

Marie Volkers' Dutch and Int. Ch. Beagold Black Moses. (Several generations of black puppies that have stayed black into adulthood.)

Suzanne Moorhouse's Ch. Willowmead Perfect Lady. (A beautiful example of the lovely brown colour.)

Born-black from strong black lines; those that change to slate
With slate and the black puppies there will be no pigmentation problems, if both are from dominantly dark parents and similarly coloured grandparents. There are breeding lines that produce dark slates, ones that produce born-blacks that turn to dark grey, and ones, born-blacks that stay black all through their life (only a very few stay black). Most give grey and slate.

We have often bred our born-black, that stay black throughout their lives, to dark slate or black bitches, and we expect several in the litter to have black coats into adulthood. The dog that started our black line was Tuftine Brigadier, a working farm-bred dog that was passed for Registration by the Kennel Club after being assessed by a Championship Show Judge just before they clamped down on all second-class registrations from unregistered parents. He was mated to the very dark slate bitch Ch. Wishanger Winter Harvest (sister to Ch. Wishanger Cairnbahn), and from that mating we had a bitch called Wishanger Bridge O'Gairn who was black coated right up until she died. We mated her to our Ch. Davealex Royle Baron; this weakened the black colouring a little, as he is grey, but his dam was dark slate, and we received from Baron many other excellent qualities that we wanted in the line. We kept a black daughter, Beagold Pennyroyal. It was difficult to chose a mate suitable for her, as we wanted strong dark pigmentation. We found it in Swiss Champion Hylas von der Elsternhoh, a dog bred in Switzerland by Mrs Annie Kurzbein from a line lost here in England. Hylas was brought back by his owner, Mrs Jean Trevisan, when she returned to live here. Hylas was born black with very little white marking; although he has changed to dark slate, he retains the darkest pigmentation. The darkest puppy in the litter we called Beagold Porter Harvey; at the age of two years he was exported to Denmark, where he has continued winning and will soon be a Danish Champion.

Before he went, Beagold Porter Harvey was mated to a Baron daughter, whose sire on the dam's side was my black-and-white Beagold Buzz [Ch. Wishanger Cairnbahn (dark brown) ex Ch. Beagold Ella (black)]. Sadly, we had only three in the litter from this mating: a black-and-white bitch who had been promised to a breeder in America, a blue dog that went to Holland, and Beagold Black Camaro, the black dog that we kept. The whole litter was a study in dark pigmentation. Even the blue dog had to be seen in strong light in order to detect the blue colouring. He had dark-blue eyes and pigmentation. The other two had black eyes when young, which then turned to dark brown as they grew older. All pads were black, and nails and the inside of the mouth were as black as a Chow's.

Beagold Porter
Harvey.

Beagold Black Camaro was only used at stud once, when he mated Mr and Mrs Jones' bitch from the Edenborough line. They kept a black dog very similar to his size. Little Monty was a slow maturer, he kept his sire's colouring, had a good head, but although he won Reserve C.C. he has never made up. Whilst breeding for colour, we never lost sight of the other requirements we considered of great importance; temperament, construction, movement, etc.

With all his other attributes, Black Camaro inherited the most gorgeous expression; his immediate ancestors had the typical Beardie expression but his touched your heart when you had his soul-stirring gaze pointed in your direction. Beagold Black Camaro had strong black lines running through his pedigree, with just a smattering of brown at the great-grandsire stage. There was no dilution with blue until the great-great-grandparent. In his pedigree there were many born blacks which stayed black throughout their lives. Those which did not, were dark slate or medium grey. The black strain had to be carefully bred for; very little dilution by light grey, blue or light brown would be needed to change the pattern to one in which there could be born black puppies but they would change to light colours as they grew older. Every so often there could be a throwback to black, but the more light colouring that was introduced would soon end the strong black line.

Puppies from Beagold Porter Harvey out of Beagold Cymbal (dark slate) were sold and in their turn were mated back to descendants of Beagold Buzz (black) so again producing strong black colour with the attractive black pigment to match.

The born-black that will stay dark slate are usually from parents one or both of which are dark slate. Dark slate is a dominant colour in the Beardie. The change to slate is not quite so noticeable at an early age, as is the change to, say, silver-grey. It may be thought that the puppy will stay black all through his life, since the change to slate does not start until the puppy is about a year old. Such puppies look rather comical, with a sort of tattered appearance; no amount of grooming will make them sleek. The coat goes through all sorts of dark grey shades, and eventually ends up, at the age of about two years, at the colour that it will stay. I have noticed that many slate-coloured dogs have exceptionally harsh coats with thick undercoats, obviously passed down pure from the early ancestors who had to have the correct coat to survive in the job they were bred for. Another type of dark-slate coat stays even-coloured all over the body with lighter grey only on the 'trousers'; where the white meets up with the dark-grey colouring, there is a fawn tinge; this is what is left when a born-black puppy has tri-colour markings.

Coat texture in relation to colour
I cannot say that I associate any particular texture of coat with a particular colour. There are soft-coated and harsh-coated Beardies in all colours. Too much bathing will soften a coat, and dry it so that the first brushing after the bathing will bring out handfuls of hair. But good food (with added vitamin supplements) keeps the coat gleaming and healthy, and extra brushing or combing have no effect whatsoever on the length or texture. It is only when the dog is allowed to get matted, or exercised where brambles can rip at the coat, or is allowed to play in sea water, that the coat is damaged.

Some lines of our breed never seem to be out of coat; a very profuse coat starts to grow when puppies are eight weeks; during the first year it continues to get more depth and length; the usual moult comes and goes without the pup ever looking leggy or short of coat; at Junior stage, the coat only adds to its depth and length; finally the transition into adulthood comes in un-noticed. But other lines drop their coat at a change in the weather, go through an ugly leggy stage, and never seem to be in full bloom. No particular colour can be singled out. (I used to think that browns spent more time in coat than out of coat, but recently I have noticed some very sparse-coated browns.)

Chris and Ken Whybrow's Teddy Brown at Beagold. (He always retained his gorgeous brown colouring.)

Born-dark-brown puppies that will stay dark brown
Having established five generations of strong black lines, we have started to incorporate the characteristic with the gorgeous dark-brown colour of that famous dark-brown Ch. Wishanger Cairnbahn. This was an unchartered area for us to enter, but looking around at the brown Beardies being shown, we were able to pick out his descendants each time, and were amazed how few breeders were taking advantage of perpetuating this line. He also had a special harsh texture of coat, dark-brown eyes, and when the early Standard was discussed they must have used him as a guide for the colour 'reddish-fawn', which is now fast disappearing. During the years when Ch. Wishanger Cairnbahn was being exhibited, most of the early breeders rushed to take full advantage of this handsome dog; he produced some outstanding puppies which carried his wealth of coat, his good temperament, and his dark pigment, (whether in born-black or born-brown puppies). When Cairnbahn died his son Wishanger Cairngarroch was still being shown; unfortunately he was very rarely used at stud, although he had many of the attributes of his sire. The reason was that he was a very lively dog and loved everyone; his behaviour

in the show ring was like a circus act, enjoyable for everyone to watch, but not so for his handler and owner. He played away his chances of winning the necessary C.C.s, and consequently those that chose their blood lines only from Champions and popular winning dogs over-looked the in-bred son. Barry Diamond mated his dog Cairngarroch [Ch. Wishanger Cairnbahn (dark brown) ex Ch. Wishanger Winter Harvest: brother/sister mating] to his own bitch Ch. Andrake Black Diamond [Ch. Davealex Royle Brigadier ex Osmart Black Bess] and here again the strong reddish-fawn colour has been repeated in part of the litter. Cairngarroch is no longer with us, he died at the ripe old age of thirteen, and to the end he resembled his illustrious sire more than ever with his mahogany dark brown coat of harsh texture.

These reddish-brown Beardies stand out in the show ring; their pigmentation is dark brown, and the iris of their eyes is the brown of their coat. Even their pads and nails are brown. Sadly they are getting fewer and fewer in numbers and the strong colour is being lost. Our descendant from that line, Peter McKenzie at Beagold was the darkest brown at birth, and even during the change of coat at ten months only went a fraction lighter down the length of his back, as the puppy coat disappeared to be replaced by a sleeker-textured, not quite so fluffy, darker coat. His ears stayed dark brown, but the rest of his body is of solid brown, never shading like *café au lait*. Although pig-mentation is strong and colour good in most of the dark-browns from this line, there are puppies born with pink spots on the nose. This is not easy to explain away, as the eye rims, mouth and the rest of the nose are strongly coloured. The line-bred son of Ch. Wishanger Cairnbahn that we owned several years ago, Beagold Haresfoot Cof-fee, always had a pink spot on the side of his nose, similar to his sire when he was young, but his pigment and coat colour were excellent. He never went through the stage when his coat paled, even when he was a junior. His coat was harsh and no amount of grooming would make him look tidy; the slightest breeze would ruffle it, and conse-quently seemed to alter his excellent outline. There are some very dark brown Beardies with a softer but good-textured coat, coats that are straight but remain body hugging. These look very beautiful in the show ring. Two of the Beardies that I have admired are Ch. Pepperland Lyric John at Potterdale, and Suzanne Moorhouse's Ch. Willowmead Perfect Lady (see photographs).

Born-blue and born-fawn

Many of the puppies born blue have not been recognised as such, and registered as 'grey'. Fawn-born puppies have been registered as light brown. This mis-registering is a pity, as these two colours are very attractive in their own right, and so completely different. The born-blue has a distinct blue colouring, with a blue nose and eye rims, and is blue around the mouth; when older, they should have lovely grey or blue eyes to match (not the china blue of the wall-eye – which is a fault – but a soft blue grey). The blue coat in full bloom is beautiful, and of usually good texture. The dog who excelled in all these attributes, giving the blue a glamorous image, was Ch. Edenborough Blue Bracken. None of his pigmentation faded; to the end of his days he retained his beautiful blue coat. Many blues lose the blue sheen of their coat at middle age; they do, however, retain their blue-grey pigment and eye colour, and this is the only way they can be recognised. The coat usually changes to grey.

Mr and Mrs Fletcher's fawn bitch Ch. Romalia Rafaelle.

I was once judging in Finland and had to give a Judge's critique in the ring. The dog in front of me could have been blue or grey, but his eyes were brown. His pigment was dark, but could have been verging on blue. I asked the owner, 'Is your dog blue or grey?'. She replied that she thought he was blue but was not sure. I suggested to her that she be sure, because if it was a born-black, now grey, it could have brown eyes; but if it was a born-blue, it should not have brown eyes, but eyes to tone with coat She decided there and then it was not blue but born-black.

In a litter of born-black puppies that I had in 1964, there was one

Ian Copus' Ch.
Kimrand Carousel
(a well known blue
bitch).

dog that stood out as completely different in colour to the others; his colour was that of a baby mouse. I had never come across a blue before, and asked the one or two breeders that had bred, at that time, more Beardies, if he could be a 'sport'. They could not give me any information on the colour, so he remained a mystery, until I was able to discover for myself that there were different shades of blue cropping up every so often in the breed. I did not keep him (although he was very attractive) because I had heard a rumour that blues automatically threw whites and smooths (of, course, completely incorrect).

The blue coat is a solid colour; during the moult there is very little change in colour and shading. The same applies to fawn.

The born-fawn has a coat colour like pink champagne; if there is white marking, it blends in with the fawn coat, and cannot be seen as the dogs get older. The eye is pale fawn, but should not detract from the dog's show-worthiness if it matches the coat. Pigment should not be pink, but light fawn. Many light-brown puppies born are registered as fawn, but when you have seen a true born-fawn you can not mistake it for any other colour.

It is a pity that the fawn colour has not become so popular as the blue. The pale colour of the fawn eye might be the reason; certainly it is not the colour of the coat, because the full-coated fawn is a beautiful sight, and stands out so noticeably against the popular greys.

Only one or two born fawn Beardies have reached the heights.

Judges that do not know will argue with the owners in the ring that the dog is light brown, or consider it to be wishy-washy brown. Mr and Mrs Fletcher's fawn bitch Ch. Romalia Rafaelle is the first Fawn Champion. She is beautifully constructed, and being any other colour would have have been made up before now. Mr and Mrs Webb's fawn bitch Stansuza Alexia has done quite a bit of winning, but is often mistaken for light brown. I saw her as a pup, and she stood out as fawn against her brown litter brothers. Sue Brown has mated her brown stud dog Hamtune Hillsider Hal to her fawn bitch Zorisaan Winter Bellarina; the whole litter was brown and fawn, but the brown puppies were so dark brown in colour, not at all diluted by their fawn dam.

Tri-colours and others
I find tri-colour puppies most attractive. They can be found only in one or two lines, and might give the novice breeder a bit of a shock, as they are not generally known about. A tri-colour puppy is born with usual collie markings of black-or-brown, and white, but between the colour and the white is an edging of light or dark fawn; when the puppy grows its longer coat the fawn is hardly distinguishable, other than fawn spots over the eyebrows, on the chest and under the tail; finally, as the coat changes in the adult, the fawn colour usually disappears completely.

Brown-to-brown mating
This mating has been done quite recently with success. To my surprise, I have seen in part of the litter even darker browns than the parents; I have not, however, been able to assess the experiment in the whole litter. There has also only been time for the first generation to show the excellent pigmentation and colour; careful planned breeding with the first generation could prove a success in the second, and from then on. From past experience, I do not think the success will continue if blue-coloured dogs are brought into the experiment.

The brown-to-brown matings have also been with dark-brown Beardies. I have not seen the very light brown with poor pigment have any other than weaker-coloured puppies. Unmistakable signs of colour paling shows when the hair is parted, and pale skin with a first growth of nearly-white hair shows beneath the darker brown. Any sign of pink lips or eye-rims at an early age bodes ill for the future. Pigment may improve for a short while, but there is every chance that it will completely disappear as a puppy becomes an adult.

A very pale-coated bitch with complete loss of pigment was once brought to my born-black Beagold Buzz. At first I was going to refuse to allow the mating, but looking at her pedigree, I could see that she had blue and brown parents. This would be a golden opportunity to prove my theory that blue would dilute colour, and that a single dark-brown was insufficient. With the cooperation of the owner, I was able to see the resulting litter several times before they were sold. The whole litter had strong colour at birth; pigmentation came quite quickly in five, and three were born with nearly completely covered black noses (they were the ones that resembled the sire in colour and marking). With Ch. Wishanger Cairnbahn as the grandsire on the sire's side, I expected that the browns would be dark, but they were not as dark as I had hoped. The three black-and-white continued to show strong colour up to eight weeks; the browns paled noticeably, and one was losing pigment around its eyes and mouth. There had been a fair amount of success in the exercise; it proved that mating to a black dog to improve colour was not enough. Only two of the puppies continued with dark-slate coats throughout their lives; the others got even paler as they grew older.

White puppies and mis-marks
In a 1964 litter of eight puppies, two were mis-marked; one badly so, the other with large black patches over one eye and white over the other. The rest of the litter was evenly marked, and beautifully dark in colour. These remained dark slate throughout their lives and disproved the idea of white mis-marks being born in pale-coloured litters. The sire was Wishanger Scots Fir, and the dam was my Ch. Beagold Ella. Ella was mated to several other dogs but never had another mis-mark. None of her progeny in this country produced mis-marks, but a great-grandson that was sent over to Canada was mated to a bitch and there were two mis-marks in that litter.

I do not find the mis-mark patchy colouring at all attractive. It looks so completely foreign in the breed. The complete white, however, with perhaps black ears or even just black around the eyes, is an attractive colour, certainly not unsightly. I should personally be wary about using such a bitch for breeding; a small mis-marking showing on any part of the bitch could give the impression that mis-marking is close in her breeding.

In America they have an all-white Champion; she is not an albino as she has dark eyes and a little black around her face, but using her as a brood bitch is sure to produce more mis-mark puppies, instead of stamping out the problem.

Most breeders have their likes and dislikes in colour. Colours take their turn at being popular in the show ring, and they should definitely not be the final criterion when a judge is making a final choice from the winning line-up. It is the variety of colour that makes the breed so interesting. In a recent single litter, we had fawn, blue, brown, and black. This does not occur very often, and we are very proud of our bitch – and of course, the stud dog.

Confusion arises over the colour of the eyes; the Standard asks for 'Eyes toning with coat colour', so the four coat colours, with the in-between colours taken into account, should have dark brown eyes with black, dark slate, and dark grey coat. Light-grey-coated Beardies can have lighter eyes. The brown-coated Bearded should have brown eyes, the light brown can have lighter shades. The light-fawn-coated can have pale fawn eyes. The blue-pigmented and blue-coated Beardies should have dove-grey-blue eyes. Some have light brown, and to be hypercritical that is incorrect. Also the wall-eye, or china-blue eye, is not allowed in the Standard; there are of course Bearded Collies who have wall-eyes and they should be sold as pets as there is nothing at all wrong with them – this characteristic is just not allowed in the Standard for show dogs. Blue Merle Rough Collies, Smooth Collies, Shelties etc., can have wall-eyes, so it is sad that we are not allowed them.

9 Training for the Show Ring; Showing

Training

Training your puppy for the show ring should start at a very early age. The puppy need be only four weeks old when you first handle it; this can be done while playing with and checking over the litter. It is quite natural to stand the pup to assess its good points. Hold the pup gently under the chin with your right hand, and very carefully lift the puppy's front legs off the ground, very slightly, with your left hand under his brisket (chest). His front legs should dangle loosely; he will stretch out to reach the ground and land on his toes. This will teach the pup to stand up on his toes later without support. Say 'Stand' all the while at the beginning. The pup will not mind; it will seem like a game, and after a second he can return to his litter mates in play.

As the puppy gets older, the stand exercise should last a little longer; the handler should give many soft words of praise, and with gentle handling move and place legs and tail. Always stroke the tail down, and say 'Tail down', right from the beginning. (Tail position is a problem in our breed; the natural liveliness of the Beardie shows when he flies his tail, but it spoils the outline, especially if there is a noticeable drop off at the croup.) Once the tail has been held up and over the back (and sometimes even in a tight curl) and the habit of holding it there is established, it is very difficult – sometimes impossible – to correct this fault.

We play a tape recorder throughout the day to accustom the dog to noise and distractions. Included in the tape are banging pans, doors slamming, low-flying planes, and quite a bit of hand clapping. Several of the Championship Show grounds are right next to airports (the worst is Windsor, where Concorde flies quite low over the rings). If the dog is not used to these noises, it can easily be put off, or even spoilt for other shows.

Eventually, the pup will stand alone for several minutes; this is the first hurdle overcome. The next time, it can be for longer, and soon the pup will stand for as long as he is asked. Once his confidence is gained, he will allow you to position his legs, and allow another person to go over him without moving, just wagging his tail to show

Setting up an eleven-week-old pup. Hold the head in the correct position, and place the hocks so that the pup can stand comfortably. The front legs should be placed showing the correct slope of the shoulder. The tail is down, and the topline level. Command the pup to 'Staaand'.

A dog standing in a natural stance.

friendliness. Some owners prefer to walk a dog into a pose using titbits for encouragement; others pick their dogs up with a hand under the brisket, dropping the front legs straight down, and then arrange the back legs (see photograph). Any procedure that is used in order to present your Beardie to look more appealing to the judge is the method that you should adopt and practise at home when the puppy is young and a willing learner. Because you train your puppy to accept positioning, it does not follow that you must *continue* placing his legs. With regular training session he will automatically stand in the correct position naturally; most judges are very impressed to see a natural stance rather than a strung-up or held-up dog that looks as if it will topple over if the leash is dropped, or if your knee is moved away.

Train puppies three times a day if possible, prior to feeding times (after they have eaten, they quickly lose interest and want to sleep). The sessions should last about ten minutes, and include walking the pup on the lead on different surfaces (carpet, lino etc.) – in fact under all sorts of different conditions. How often do you see a six-month-old dog encountering the slippery floor of a hall for the first time refusing to move, especially if he has been shown outside on grass throughout the summer months?

For his first appearance in the show ring, the youngster will need encouragement and just a little reminder that all that training was for this great day. Stand slightly over him; hold his head up, by placing your right hand under his chin, if you think he is going to sit (which is what often happens just when the judge is looking your way). Gently caress him under his stomach; say 'Staaaand!' Never attempt to raise the puppy with your hand under his stomach; if this is done often, it makes him roach (i.e. arch his back); his tummy is tender, and he will always draw away from a not-too-gentle hand, thus developing strong tummy muscles that will make him look tucked up.

After several training sessions, in which the pup has been placed in the correct position, the pup is now ready to stand naturally on the command 'Staaand'.

(a)   (b)

Correct and incorrect holds for positioning Beardies for training for show. (a) is correct. The right hand is under the dog's muzzle, and the left lifts the dog gently up on to its toes. (b) is incorrect. The left hand, lifting the dog by his stomach will eventually encourage it to roach its topline.

Showing

What helps a puppy more than anything else on his first showing is being put in the car with older dogs who know the procedure. The walk to the show ring from the car park can be a traumatic experience (especially in the queue to get into the venue), but a puppy will readily copy an older dog's acceptance of the situation. He will also watch him jump up onto his benches, and follow him, but let him stay a short while, and *then* transfer him to his own bench.

It is so important that a dog is encouraged to accept the bench at a show; this should be regarded as his haven, where he will be comfortably settled with his owner's belongings, happy to be left for just a little while on his own to guard and rest while his owner is away for one reason or another. I have seen so many Beardies allowed to lie on the floor or off the bench because the owner is unable to get them on to the bench. In this situation, they could well be in everyone's way, trodden on and even attacked by dogs passing by. It should be no effort or problem for the dog new to the show to jump up on his bench; if he is reluctant then he could be lifted up.

Next, at his first show, he will have to accustom himself to the various noises; that is what all the hours of training have been for. A collapsing bench, ring-number board flapping in wind, applause (in particular clapping) may all alarm. Beardies react more than any other breed to applause: the applause that heralds a winner of the Best of Breed in another ring can trigger off the Beardies immediately to jump and bark; a chain reaction may then start through the show ground. It is not bad sportsmanship when no applause is made for the winners at Beardie Shows; exhibitors simply know that it would be bedlam if they showed their approval of a particular good win.

We advise a fine check-chain, or slip collar and leash, for training while the puppy is young. As the chain tends to cut the coat around the neck, it is best to keep it solely for the time spent in training. If the puppy is easy to train we use a fine roll collar and leash. The Beardie is a very lively dog, and needs more control than an all-in-one nylon slip lead, where the part that goes around the dog's neck can be enlarged or made smaller with a movable clasp, can provide. Such leads can be used when the puppy is trained, but firm and safe control is needed while it is being trained.

One of the problems that seems to develop quite often in Beardies is that a normally low-set tail can be carried up and over the back when the pup is excited (see page 91). If this is allowed to continue, without immediate checking, it becomes a habit. We have found that young puppies will play a game in a yard where they pull and tug to try to carry a broom: carrying this weight, they balance themselves by putting their tails down. We also watch the pups at meal times; those that raise their tails up and over their backs need them gently pushed down. With contact on their rump, say 'Tail down'. Certainly it takes time, regular training, and no let up on the 'Tail down'.

With the tail problem solved, there is the 'hold head up on the move' problem to cope with. The working sheepdog does his work with his head held level with his back in a crouching position; although this might be the right stand for working dog, it is not working when it is being shown, and the rather hangdog appearance when the head is held lower than the topline does not look so attractive. Only a little amount of encouragement is needed to get the dog to raise his head on the move; the natural liveliness of a breed which wants to see everything, and the desire to look up into yout face for approval, will keep the head up, whilst the dog will move just as well. I have watched Mr Cosme's training sessions; with the dog standing beside him, he gently caresses the dog, saying, 'Stand, good boy; head up and tail down, good boy'. This he repeats several times; he then moves the dog with the same words of encouragement.

So many Beardie owners chose to plunge straight into the Championship Show ring with their new puppy (usually untrained), before they have ever been to any type of show. It is not surprising that owner and dog are completely confused. The owner will have built up a picture in his or her mind about the winning capabilities of the puppy; now, having put it to the test, the disappointment when not placed in the winners line-up is enough to discourage him or her from ever entering a show ring again. I have met many disgruntled first-time exhibitors who misconstrue the reason for the regular show-goers always winning.

In the early days of showing, it was usual practice for the beginner to start at Matches and Exemption Shows; then came Sanction and Limited Shows. Once you had served your apprenticeship, learning and winning at these small shows, you took the exciting step of entering the nearest Open Show. A Very Highly Commended win at an Open Show was greatly prized; your aim was to win a red card; when this great day came, you went into the ring with all the other unbeaten dogs. Very few aspired to Championship Shows before winning well at Open Shows; they made sure that they had a well-trained show dog, capable of taking his place with equally disciplined others. The regular show-goers climbed the ladder step by step. By the time they won a first-prize card, they accepted with a rather blasé air, even though they might be secretly bubbling with excitement inside.

Even if you have jumped in straightaway, and entered a Championship Show, it is worthwhile going to Exemption, Sanction or Limited Shows. There you will meet a variety of dog owners all new to the show world like yourself; you are there to learn and enjoy yourselves; in fact many of you will be taking your first steps into the show world. There is a happy relaxed atmosphere; competition is not so keen. Go with the idea that you are there to enjoy yourself, and that you will be satisfied if your dog behaves; look on the show as a training ground. If you do not count on winning, what a delightful surprise it is if you do win a card (especially now that the Exemption Shows have as many as twenty or thirty dogs in a class). If you have doubts about your dog settling down before the Judge looks at him, it is best to get to the end of the line-up; your dog will then have accustomed himself to the other dogs, by the time the Judge is ready to look at him.

Do not allow your dog to wander and annoy other exhibits; do not let him crowd the person in front, or let him move up and hide the dog moving ahead of you. Similarly, do not allow the person behind to crowd you. Watch for directions from the Steward, and Judge; be sure to react immediately if the Judge wishes to see you move your dog again. Most judges ask you first to move your dog in a straight line up and back, and then to move with your dog in a triangle. Fix your eye on one point of the ring and go straight to it; that allows the Judge to assess your dog's back movement; then move straight across the ring so that the Judge can see your dog's side gait, and whether he is striding out as he should, holding a level topline, and holding his tail in the correct position. The last part of the triangle will be coming in a straight line towards the Judge; this allows him to see if

The dog's pace matches that of his handler. He is moving on a loose lead, showing a natural and balanced movement.

the dog is walking with a hackney motion, or paddling, or pin-toeing. Sometimes the Judge likes to see a final run-round before placing the winners in order; never imagine that you can ease up and relax, wherever you are placed, until you receive your prize card.

Your philosophy should be: 'My aim in bringing my Beardie to a dog show is to get the opinion of the Judge on my dog's good and bad points. I will take my placing gracefully, and remember that this is only one Judge's opinion – the next Judge might find in my dog all the points he is looking for and place it higher, or else place it nowhere. I will enter the ring to perform as a handler, and concentrate completely on the job in hand and my dog. Everyone likes to be placed first, but it is better to be concerned with the joint effort rather than the actual placing.'

Mr Tom Horner, the Judge, with Mr Felix Cosme and Ch. Davealex Royle Baron.

If you have encouraged your dog to jump up on to a low table to be groomed, the benches at shows will hold no problems for it. Many people prefer not to use a bench chain, as the constant jangle of the chain against the metal partition is a bit unnerving for a young dog. Most dogs appreciate a blanket, rug or towel put down on the wooden bench so that they can rest in comfort while they are waiting.

It is dangerous to leave a dog on a long lead on the bench; an inquisitive young dog will try to investigate the dog benched next to him, or go to the limit of the lead and, unless he is rescued quickly, get strangled as he struggles half-on and half-off the bench. Slip chains are equally dangerous; an active dog can get his legs caught as he moves around. It is advisable not to leave any dog alone for more than a few minutes. (It has become the practice now to ask neighbours to watch and guard the dogs if it is necessary for the owner to be away for any length of time.)

Most Beardies appreciate a small meal, and several drinks while they are at a show, especially if they have come a long way. They

Mrs Glynis
Chambers handling
Beagold Royal
Fortune (Grandson
of Ch. Davealex
Royle Baron).

should also be taken off their benches for exercise at regular intervals, and especially before they are taken into the ring. The indoor shows provide an exercise and grooming room; the outside shows usually have acres of grassland surrounding the tents.

However often you take your puppy through training sessions at home, such sessions do not provide the atmosphere and distractions that he will encounter at shows; to further his education, join one of the local dog show handling classes. Only a few visits will be needed before you can enter your first show with confidence that your puppy will behave in all situations. As I suggested in a previous chapter, it is advisable to start at the bottom of the show 'hierarchy' and work your way up a step at a time: Matches, Exemption Shows, Primary Shows, Sanction and Limited, then Open and finally (reaching your goal), Championship Shows. If you win a first at a Championship Show in the qualifying classes, you and your dog are qualified to exhibit at Cruft's.

Types of Show

Exemption Shows. These entries can be made on the day of the show. You will be required to fill in a small entry form giving the puppy's age, its name, and your name and address. 'Exemption' means that although the show organisers need a licence, and permission from the Kennel Club to run the show, it is 'exempt' from most of the Kennel Club rules. You do not need to own a pedigree or a Registered dog to compete. There is very little chance of a cross-bred winning in the four Show classes, usually Puppy (dog or bitch, six months to one year), Non-Sporting, Sporting, and Open. Some top-quality show-winning dogs are now taken to Exemption Shows for training, and these take all the prizes. There is much more likelihood of a cross-bred winning in the many Novelty Classes on offer, like 'the dog the judge would most like to take home', and 'The best-condition dog or bitch'. These shows are wonderful training grounds for all dogs, and the atmosphere of friendly rivalry is not found in any of the other shows.

Primary Shows. Only members of the Association, Club or Society may compete. These shows are usually held on Saturday or Sunday after 2 p.m. or in the evening after 5 p.m. There will be only 8 classes and the highest which may be scheduled is Maiden. Here, as in the Exemption Show, entries can be taken on the day of the show. This is another show that caters mainly for newcomers, and a marvellous opportunity for young puppies to come out.

Limited and Sanction Shows. You must become a member of the Club concerned to exhibit at these shows. The membership fee is quite small, and entitles you to enter their three shows held during the year, and attend the twelve matches, held one a month. The fee also entitles you to win the many Challenge cups and trophies which will be on offer at every show, donated by past and present members for a particular breed. The friendly atmosphere is certainly found at these shows, but a little more keen competitive spirit is present, too. 'Limit' means that the show is limited to members; there are more breed classes, with about half of the classes for Variety entries. Challenge Certificate winners cannot enter the show, but the classification goes up to Limit and Open Classes for the dogs that are eligible for entry in those classes.

The added incentive to belong to a Club or Association that runs Limited Shows is the opportunity to win a silver trophy, a prize card and prize money, and sometimes a rosette; such things are a wonderful boost to our ego if you are just starting as an exhibitor.

Sanction Shows are usually held in the evenings, mainly during the winter, and have no more than twenty-five classes of Varieties; no special breed classes are allowed.

Open Shows. During the summer there are many Open Shows, sometimes held in conjunction with agriculture shows, which can offer interest for the rest of the family. 'Open' means open to all dogs, including Champions. Throughout the summer months, there are shows of all types to choose from every week. Wet-weather accommodation is usually in the form of large marquees, with benches for the dogs when they are not being shown in the rings. In the winter they are held in halls and large community centres, in most large towns. Here you will be offered classes for Bearded Collies, with either an all-round judge, or a breed-specialist judge. A first win at an Open Show gives you one point to count towards the Junior Warrant, if that win is in a breed class. A first win at a Championship Show gives you three points. Your dog must win 25 points before he reaches the age of 18 months to gain the Junior Warrant. The first bitch ever to win her Junior Warrant was Miss Mary Partridge's Ch. Wishanger Winter Harvest. Since then there have been many. It is sad to say that there is little credit or publicity given to these winners; personally I think it is most difficult to win the necessary points, particularly in our breed. So many Beardies mature late, and have to compete against the few very early maturers, who have a wealth of coat, sometimes covering a very immature body.

At Open Shows, there are classes like A.V. Pastoral, A.V. Working, and Non-Sporting, as well as breed classes. We usually enter, as this gives us an opportunity of showing under a different judge at the same show.

Championship Shows. With the increase of Registrations in our breed, 30 sets of tickets were offered to us in 1985, plus 3 sets for the three Club Shows. The first Championship Show of the year is Crufts, followed by Manchester, Scottish Breeds Canine Club, W.E.L.K.S.,

Front view showing how the handler controls the dog without too much handling.

Back view showing good hocks and tail set.

The view the judge has when the dog is presented by the handler kneeling down behind.

The view from the handler's side, showing how he gently controls the dog to keep his head up, and holds the lead loosely.

Bath, Birmingham (Nat.), S.K.C., Southern Counties, Three Counties, Border Union, Blackpool, Windsor, Paignton, South Wales K.A., East of England A.S., Leeds, Bournemouth, Welsh K.C., S.K.C. Leicester, Birmingham City, Darlington, Richmond, Belfast, Midland Counties, Driffield, L.K.A., National Working Breeds, and Working Breeds of Wales.

The entry fee includes the benching fee, and is usually about £6.00

A corner of the show ring, with the Open Dog Class of the Darlington Championship Show. Specialist Breed Judge Mr Barry Diamond watches Mr Felix Cosme moving Ch. Edenborough Star Turn at Beagold.

for each dog. Every year it gets more difficult to qualify for entry to Cruft's. At the moment you have to win a first Prize in Minor Puppy, Puppy, Junior, Post Graduate, Limit or Open; Reserve C.C. winners and C.C. winners can enter, Champions automatically qualify. The qualifying rules as they stand are all in favour of the top dogs in our breed, giving very little chance to our puppies and slow maturers. I agree the Minor Puppy class should be included as a qualifying class as we have so many very young pups coming along, and the thousands of visitors to Cruft's mainly come to see the young stock and potential winners.

At Championship Shows you will meet real competition; the classes are very large, and when you look around you will wonder to yourself whatever made you think that your young dog was so special and better in so many respects than the rest. The time of judging will be mentioned in the Schedule and Catalogue, and although you might have brought your dog groomed and clean, you will notice all around that the other exhibitors are putting the finishing touches to their well-groomed dogs. First in the ring will be 'Minor Puppy Dog' (puppy dogs from 6 months to 9 months).

When the Class for which you are entered comes, you make your way to the ring, to be ready to take your place in the line-up for the Steward to check your number. Most judges get the puppies walking around the ring to start with, then call each one individually into the centre for further inspection. This is where all your training comes to good use, especially if the pup stands still while the Judge goes over him. Most young pups are forgiven if they welcome the Judge, but any boisterous behaviour should not be encouraged. After the Judge has gone over all the exhibits, he will pick out his five winners; they may not be placed in order, but you will be able to stand your dog in the line up while the Steward thanks the rest of the exhibitors as they leave the ring. The Judge may then ask the five to take their dogs around the ring again. He will then pick out his winners in order of merit. Wherever you are in that line-up you will receive a prize card, and sometimes prize money. Should you be first, you will be called in when all the dogs have been judged in subsequent classes, to compete with the unbeaten dogs for the Challenge Certificate. The Reserve C.C. will go to the second best.

The bitches are then called into the ring to be judged, and the same procedure is followed. the C.C. winning bitch then competes with the C.C. winning dog for Best of Breed. When the dog or bitch win three Challenge Certificates under three different judges, so long as they are over the age of one year, they can be called Champion. If a dog is under the age of one year, he cannot be acclaimed as a Champion until he wins a Challenge Certificate after his first Birthday.

The Best of Breed winner then has to compete against all the other breeds in the Working Group. Over the last few years many Bearded Collies have won this Group, or been Reserve in it. This gives some indication of the improved quality of our breed. Should the Beardie win the Working Group, he then takes his place with the other Group winners for the Best in Show award. Only a few Beardies have reached these dizzy heights at Championship Shows. It is a great achievement to have won under the Breed Judge, then another judge for the Working Group, and then a different Judge for Best in Show.

Entries close at most shows from three weeks to a month before the show. The Schedules can be obtained from the Secretary of the Society or Association. The advertisement for the show will be in the dog magazines or in the *Kennel Gazette*, which can be bought only from the Kennel Club. Regular showgoers receive their Schedules automatically through the post.

When you have been going to shows regularly, and at every show your dog has been placed in the winning line-up – first, second or third – it is worth persevering further. Of course he may have his off days, but as he grows older and wins through to Open Classes, there is every chance that eventually he will be placed above all the others and gain his first Challenge Certificate. The following C.C.s will never be quite such exciting wins. Even when you gain the third and the title, your first C.C. win will remain forever in your mind as the hurdle you had never dared hope to surmount.

Judging
Those that wish eventually to become a judge should take the same course as showing, and start right at the bottom. Start judging at Matches, and then at Exemption Shows, to gain the experience of being on your own in the ring where you have to make the correct decision as to the relative merits of the dogs in front of you. Of course there must be several years of show-going behind you, with experience in all sorts of shows. If you have stewarded several times, that experience is a great help.

Showing is an expensive game now, and after paying for their entry, exhibitors expect to have their dogs assessed in a professional manner. A judge who selects casually will not draw a good entry the next time around. No one expects to win all the time, and so long as you are satisfied that it was your dog the judge found fault with and did not place, rather than that the dogs who were placed in the winning line-up belonged to his friends, then you take his decisions with good grace, and think to yourself 'Another day, another show, another Judge'.

When you are first invited to judge our breed, you should have already gained 'ring confidence', if not the actual experience of judging. It should be a rule that a would-be judge has bred and shown the Bearded Collie for several years, or if an all-round judge, they should have at least shown some interest in our breed, and been giving C.C.s in other breeds for many years.

When you are judging for the first time, you should forget the faces at the other end of the lead, and enjoy yourself concentrating on the dogs. Remember, your decision is final; you want to be proud of your winners. They might not be the type you breed yourself, but they should answer the description in the Standard. They might not be the colour you prefer or favour, or wish to own, but that is not the point in question; they must be, in your opinion, good specimens of the Breed as laid down by the Standard.

It is advisable to judge many times at Open Show level before allowing your name to go forward for the Championship Show list. The Kennel Club have the final say whether you are accepted or not, but you must be confident that you have the knowledge and the ability to assess the dogs standing before you.

The Breed Clubs all have Judging Lists, with your qualifications as well as your name to be included. This is an excellent idea, and makes sure that unqualified people who try to come in by the back door soon find that door closed when they are called upon to complete the Questionnaire for the Kennel Club's final decision.

If you have intentions of eventually taking up judging it is wise to keep a record of the shows, classes, and numbers that you have judged. It is very easy to forget if it is several years since you qualified to give C.C.s. Personally I enjoy judging very much, and after serving many years of apprenticeship in the dog game, I feel confident to judge all breeds.

It is a great pleasure to place your final winners for Best in Show, Reserve Best in Show and Best Opposite Sex, then to be told that these placings are one of many that the exhibits have received in their show career. When I judged in Norway, and found my Best in Show from the Cocker Spaniel B.O.B. winner, I was then told that that was his fourth best in Show, this was a great feeling of satisfaction and achievement.

10 Advertising and Selling Your Beardie Pups

Breeders of litters of Beardies will need to use several means of contacting sales prospects, especially if situated in an out-of-the-way area and having never advertised before. If they belong to the local branch of the Bearded Collie Club, or go to local shows, they can spread the word that they have a litter for sale, but without such contacts, it is best to start advertising the puppies for sale when they are about five or six weeks old. Many dog owners or would-be dog owners scan the local papers that have a 'Dogs for Sale' column. Dogs of all breeds are advertised every week in the magazines *Dog World* and *Our Dogs*, but these are specialist papers, and in most places it is impossible to just call in at a newspaper shop and buy one of these: they have to be ordered. It is in these magazines that the show exhibitors, and those intending to show, will find what they are looking for.

When advertising in the Press, insert just the barest details; if the buyer reads something he likes, he will contact you for further information. For example: 'Bearded Collie puppies for sale. Sire Ch. Mr. Jones, Dam Ch. Sweet Lady. Browns and Blacks. Dogs and bitches. One or two show potential. Reasonably priced. Tel. Golders 888. Mrs Smith, 8 The Rise, Town, County.'

If you intend to keep one of the litter, do not show it. Assess the quality of each of the pups before the buyer arrives. The evenly-marked, of whatever colour, always look more attractive in the show ring; ask top price if there is one. A puppy that has uneven markings, or a head that is rather small, or a tail already tightly curled over the back, must be offered as a pet, and less charged.

Novice breeders must understand that although puppies look similar, in most respects, at this early age, they can only expect one or two puppies in each litter that will be show prospects; the rest should have the price graded. There may not be *any* good enough to show. Even when pups are line-bred from top show Champions, there is every possibility that only one or two in the litter will be as good as their parents. So many unforeseen things can happen. If you have advertised 'Top-quality show puppies', you will most certainly hear from the buyers when the pups do not live up to this description.

Many years ago I went to buy a Beagle puppy for show. I took along a friend who wanted to buy just a pet. The puppies played around on the ground before us, and I asked the breeder which were the pets and which were the show pups, and what price was she charging. She answered, 'The one you pick will be the top price, £30; that will be for show. The one your friend picks will be only £15; that will be a pet'. I told the breeder that I had changed my mind. I refused to pay for my own knowledge. Had the breeder pointed out the potential show dogs and the pets, even if I did not agree with her opinion, I would not have felt that she was using *my* knowledge to charge *me* more. So do, when the prospective buyer comes to look, have in your mind which are the best puppies and which are the not-so-good. If you have no idea, having not had the necessary experience to pick out the best, admit the fact; charge the same price for all.

Before I waste any time on an interview, I ask the prospective buyer all the relevant questions: 'Do you have a closed-in garden? Do you have children? Does your wife [husband] like dogs? Does your wife [husband] know you are buying this puppy?' I do not like selling a puppy as a birthday present if the recipient is unaware that they are receiving it, especially if during the conversation with the buyer it becomes apparent that the buyer is the one that likes dogs, and the other partner has never had one or might not accept the unsolicited present. I also point out the cost of feeding, the cost of the necessary innoculations, and the possible vet's bills. (This all brings to mind one of the funniest – in retrospect – telephone conversations that I have had with a buyer. The call itself was not too unusual. I asked the usual questions, but the answers were a trifle puzzling. To my question, 'Do you have a closed-in garden?', the answer was, 'No, but we have several acres of ground surrounding the house.' I asked if the lady of the house was away at work; the answer was, 'No, not at work but I am away quite a bit; there is always someone here at the house.' I warned about the price of food for the pup, etc.; then I invited the enquirer to come to see it. The lady arrived in a superb car; it certainly seemed that the price of the puppy and its food was not going to be a problem. When she signed the cheque for the puppy I saw, 'The Countess of Pembroke and Montgomeryshire'. The 'house' was Wilton House.)

If the buyer seems responsible, and has satisfied you with all the answers to your questions, but there seems some doubt that they can go to the price that you are asking, it may be worth bringing the price down a little, if you are quite satisfied that the buyer will give the puppy a loving and satisfactory home. But do remind the buyer that expenses do not end when he has paid for the puppy; there will be many more expenses, with food bills, injections, etc. If you doubt the buyer can afford to pay the full price, will he also be short of cash when it comes to feeding? The whole problem has to be decided at the interview, and the sale of the puppy must be secondary to the need to ensure it has a good home, adequate food, and plenty of exercise. Buyers should realise that their responsibility to the dog could extend over the next fourteen years.

I always ask the buyers to contact me if they have any problems at all; I would rather have the telephone ringing continually than the puppy suffer in any way. An upset tummy, crying at night, grooming problems, nipping, or a puppy that becomes too boisterous, can all be put right if checked in time. We feel that our responsibility does not end when the puppy leaves our kennels; we always keep enough space for it to be brought back if for some reason it has to be returned.

The larger kennels advertise regularly, and the reputation they gain from producing sound healthy puppies with excellent temperaments is good enough to bring back their old customers, and their friends. The goodwill gained from giving buyers an honest deal, and all the help you can, is advertisement in itself.

The first contact we have is usually a telephone call. Once it is established that we have a litter, and a puppy of the colour and sex that is required, then we make arrangements for the buyer to call to see the puppy. We will have sold most of the litter before they are born, so there is no need to show all the puppies; if there are three for sale of the colour and sex that has been chosen, then the buyer has a choice, but in our breed, with its variety of colours, there is not always a choice for the buyer. If the puppy is too young to be taken away, then we always ask for a deposit as a booking fee; as we have continual enquiries for puppies, we cannot afford to hold on to a puppy for six weeks with the promise that the people really want it, then when the time comes for collection they have decided against having one at that time. We do not want to force a sale by asking for the deposit though, especially if the buyer agrees to take the unwanted pup only to avoid losing his money: a buyer will give a second thought to purchasing a puppy in the first place if he thinks he might lose his deposit.

It is not possible to guarantee the health of the puppy once it leaves your premises; with improper feeding, a puppy can become ill within a few days of going to its new home. We always provide a mixed dish of food for the owner to take for its meal when it arrives home, plus the menu with all instructions for cooking, times of feeding, and types of food that the puppies have had since they were weaned. Even then mistakes can be made. One new owner could not understand why her puppy was sicking up its meal. I checked on the food she was giving it, and was assured that it was mince and biscuit meal as suggested for one meal. Eventually I found out that she was frying the mince before boiling it to make it tasty: of course the mixture was too rich. Another buyer assured me that she was sticking rigidly to the diet sheet I had given; later when I saw how enormously fat her pup had grown she did admit to giving it a bar of chocolate every day.

There are many advantages of owning a pedigree dog – and many more when that pedigree dog is a Bearded Collie. For generations the Collie has been bred to use his brain, to be a companion, and to maintain his own individuality. When selling your puppy, talk to the new owners, give them a little of the background of the breed; then they will understand and appreciate the needs of the natural fun-loving, lively and active animal that they are taking into their home. If every new owner knows exactly the type of dog they are buying, there may not be quite so many Beardies which end up on 'Rescue' schemes. Most breed clubs run a 'Rescue Scheme' so that any dog or bitch in need of a new home can be taken in temporarily until a permanent new home is found. Mrs Dorothy Jarret has run the Southern Bearded Collie Rescue scheme with success for many years. The other Clubs also have rescue schemes, but area representatives manage to rehabilitate the Beardies that needs homes in their areas. Unfortunately some Beardies are allowed to become so boisterous and uncontrollable that they have to be put down. This is a very sad situation as the Bearded Collie's character should never be so wild. On occasions, even vicious dogs arrive to be rehabilitated if possible.

11 The Kennel Club; Imports and Exports

Finally in the main part of the book, having covered the practical matters of breeding, it may be useful to summarise the necessary documents and registration, and their importance to breeders and owners.

PEDIGREE

You have decided you wish to own a pedigree dog. You have made enquiries from breeders to find out where and when there will be litters, fixed a date, and are now about to collect your first puppy. The first piece of paper you are shown is the Pedigree. It may not mean much: it is a lot of names, some written in red to denote that the dog concerned is a Champion. But even if the Pedigree is mostly in red, it does not guarantee the puppy you are about to acquire will be a Champion itself. It is only if you, the new owner, have taken trouble to see the dogs concerned that you will be able to judge the likely worth of the offspring. If you have done some homework and watched the judging in the show rings for several months, or made enquiries to learn if the bitch has produced other winning stock, or the dog has a reputation for siring top quality offspring throughout the years, and not just one litter that made its mark, then you are on the right track. Having chosen a puppy of show potential, your life will now be involved in a completely different world, the world of dog showing, and all the added cares and responsibility that goes with it. (You will also have so much paper work that you will sometimes wonder if you should not hire a secretary to deal with it all.)

Even when you purchase a pedigree dog which you intend to keep purely as a pet, you should be given a Pedigree, a menu, a receipt for your money, and information about registration at the Kennel Club. The puppy will have been registered with the Kennel Club by means of the Litter Registration form, but it might be left to you to name it and transfer it to your ownership. These forms are all very confusing and difficult to understand even for the breeder who works regularly with them.

It is essential to make sure that the litter is from registered parents, and that the Litter Registration has been applied for. It is not so long ago that the Bearded Collie was bred from farm working stock. Special permission had to be obtained from the Kennel Club to show such dogs, and the dog or bitch with unregistered parents had to be passed by a Specialist Championship Show Judge before they could be given a Class II Registration. Puppies could not be exported unless they had four generations of registered parents. In the late 1960s, Mrs Justine Warren searched Scotland and the North of England for a Bearded Collie dog to bring in new blood, and retain the working capabilities of the original Beardies. Tuftine Brigadier was found on a farm tucked away in the hills of the Border Country. He was born in 1967, and was passed for Registration by the Specialist Championship Show Judge Mr Martin in 1969.

When a puppy is given an official name, that name has to be used on every occasion that it is entered at a show. Of course you can give it a pet name, for everyday use.

The travelling box used for Bearded Collie puppies. There are wire windows on three sides, with a lift-up door on the last. It is strongly made, but in light wood.

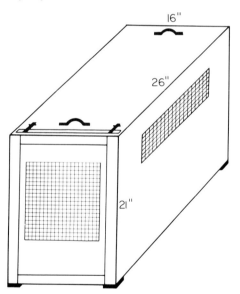

EXPORTS

The puppy that is to be exported must be registered with the K.C., and an Export Pedigree is required, which gives a three-generation ancestry of the Beardie to be exported. In the case of a male, a certificate must be signed by a veterinary surgeon saying that he has examined the dog and that both testicles are fully descended in the scrotum and apparently normal. (The puppy dog is not exported until he is well over twelve weeks of age, so this is usually just a formality; on the other hand some dogs do not mature quite so early, and then the prospective owner must send a covering letter to say that they are aware the dog is not yet entire, but they are willing to take the risk, and accept the puppy as it is.)

When the puppy is taken to the airport, it must be accompanied by a health certificate from the veterinary surgeon. Some countries insist on a rabies injection before the puppy is sent, others allow the new owners to have it done as soon as it arrives. Most countries allow dogs from Great Britain to be sent to their new owners without going first into quarantine.

It is advisable to write to the Ministry of Agriculture for information relating to export if you intend to arrange the whole business yourself. Most breeders prefer to leave the shipment in the hands of reliable shipping firms, which will attend to all the formalities, including insurance and customs, and provide a fully comprehensive transport service covering collection, transport by air and delivery to any part of the world. The travelling box is also provided; it is a specially designed and made box, light but strong. We give our shipper the measurements of the puppy (the height, from the top of its head to the ground when the puppy is sitting, and the length of the puppy from croup to nose when standing). This is to ensure that the puppy has plenty of room to move about comfortably while en route. The box that is used to take a puppy to New Zealand or Australia has to have double wire at the windows, and an ingenious attachment is included so that the puppy can be given water to drink without the sealed box being opened. Quarantine laws are strict for puppies travelling on that long journey, and once the veterinary surgeon seals the travelling box, the seals are only broken when another official collects the puppy on arrival.

The puppy is introduced to his travelling box several times before he makes the journey, so that when he is finally shut in he takes it all in his stride. I cover the floor of the specially made crate with newspaper sheets, then torn-up newspaper strips. We either take or send a plastic container with food so that he can be fed when he reaches the airport, and another container for water.

We have taken puppies up to Heathrow Airport for export to the States and the Continent. Most of the airlines request that we bring the puppy three to four hours before take off. Although we take only the Health Certificate, once we arrive at the airport there are many forms to complete. They take measurements of the box and weight of box plus puppy, a ritual which takes a good hour to perform. We have always found British Airways most helpful and efficient; there seem to be quite a few dog lovers working there. The few times we have dealt with them personally we have been very satisfied that our puppies have been looked after and speedily transported. Our agent

---

is equally happy with their capable handling of all his exports.

It is a most worrying time until the telephone call or cablegram arrives letting us know that the puppy has arrived at its destination safely. Each time we export we remember the occasion when the puppy's flight was cancelled three times because there was no heating in the cargo hold. Eventually we had to travel to the Airport to pick the puppy up from the quarantine kennels, where it had been left overnight. We refused to allow that airline to make a further booking. We have also experienced the worry of sending a puppy by a flight badly delayed by fog. We waited to see if the flight would be cancelled, and then heard the plane take off, only with the slight feeling of relief that in a few minutes the plane would be flying above the fog in a clear sky.

IMPORTS

There have been only one or two Bearded Collies imported into Great Britain. One was Mrs Jean Trevisan's Swiss Champion Hylas von der Elsternhoh (Haggis). Mrs Trevisan bought Haggis as a puppy from Mrs Kurzbein while living in Switzerland, and soon made him up to a Swiss Champion. I went to stay with the Trevisans, and we were taking Haggis into Austria to a Ch. Show there. It was neccessary then to have a vet's certificate before a dog could be admitted into an adjacent country to a show; this certificate had to be taken to the show organisers proving to them that no animals had died with rabies in the dog's home area. A cat had died of an unknown cause the night before so we could not take Haggis into Austria, but Jean Trevisan decided we would still go to the show. It was a marvellous drive, through Switzerland, then Lichenstein, and into Austria, the most wonderful scenery. Imagine my surprise when Jean gave the authorities the certificate and they gave her the prize card, Ribbons for first placing and B.O.B., and a medal that Haggis would have won if he had been there. That is the only time I have won a medal with a dog and left the dog at home.

The family then returned to England, and of course Haggis had to go into quarantine for six months. Beardies do not take kindly to being restricted in their activities for such a long time, and as Haggis was just over four years of age at that time, and had had a life of complete freedom, he took a long time to get over the very boring six months; his coat and condition were not good when he came out.

Mrs Lori Warren returned to this country from America and brought back her bitch, now called American Ch. Barnleigh Damaris. Damaris was born and shown in England. Before she was taken to the States, Damaris had been mated to my Ch. Davealex Royle Baron. Two of her puppies were sold to another American Service family who took them back to the States. Since then they have become American Champions, the dog has been used extensively at stud, while the bitch whelped several litters, nearly all becoming American Champions.

Maggie Webster brought her bitches back from their stay in Germany, where the Becobus breeding became quite well known.

12 The Modern History of the Breed

Champions and Challenge Certificate Winners which have made their mark in the breed.

Writing this book at the present stage of the Beardie's development as a breed, I feel that if the fullest information about the breed's history is not recorded now, it will be lost for ever. Consequently, I have given very full details of the leading dogs and kennels since the founding of the Bearded Collie Club.

It was in 1955 that the late Mrs Willison, owner of the Bothkennar Kennels, was instrumental in establishing the Bearded Collie Club, with 26 founder members. (Not all were actually Bearded Collie owners at that time; she was joined by friends who were interested in her efforts and wished to support her. Miss Clara Bowring was asked to become President, and members included the late Jimmie Garrow, and the late Frank Williams. As soon as the Club was formed, they applied for Challenge Certificates; however, it was not until 1959 that they had the necessary number of Registrations to qualify. Mrs Willison was then the first to make her dogs up to Champions. (*The Bearded Collie*, written by Mrs Willison and published by Foyles, gives the Bothkennar story in more detail.)

The first ever Champion was Mrs Willison's Ch. Beauty Queen of Bothkennar, then came Ch. Benjie of Bothkennar, Ch. Bravo of Bothkennar, Ch. Bronze Penny of Bothkennar and Ch. Bracken Boy of Bothkennar.

The first Bearded Collie to be exported was to the States in the early '50s (the litter was from Ridgeway Rob, out of Mrs Willison's Bra-Tawny of Bothkennar; two bitches were sent to a farm in Connecticut, but nothing has been heard of them since). Next export was a Britt of Bothkennar – Bra-Tawny of Bothkennar son, Ambassador of Bothkennar, sent to Finland. (All the Bothkennar dogs were named with an initial 'B', but as a special favour, and to mark the first import to that country, Mrs Willison named the dog 'Ambassador'.) Ambassador soon became an International Champion, and the sire of many winning dogs in that country. Mrs Willison also sent stock to Sweden,

Holland, Italy, France, South Africa, Thailand, and Switzerland.

Ch. Bobby of Bothkennar was bred by Miss Johnson and later owned by Mrs Willison. Owing to ill-health, Mrs Willison disbanded her kennels, and gave all her dogs to friends and breeders that she knew. Her kennel maid, Miss Jo Lewis, was given Ch. Bobby of Bothkennar. Shortly after, Jo and her dog left for South Africa, where he won seven more C.C.s and became their first International Champion. Jo returned to England in 1970, and married, she is now Mrs Jo Pickford. She is the owner of Ch. Osmart Black Barnacle from Penhallow, a beautiful black-and-white Beardie, and the sire of Mr Don Maskell's Ch. Penhallow Pink Panther which was Cruft's winner and B.O.B. in 1977.

Ch. Bravo of Bothkennar and Ch. Blue Bonnie of Bothkennar went to Mr and Mrs Osborne's Osmart Kennels early in 1964. In 1963 they had purchased Bluebelle of Bothkennar, who had been shown at agricultural shows regularly, but never placed – at that time she was the only Beardie being shown in the North, and consequently the Variety judges did not really know whether or not she conformed to the Breed Standard. Her first Ch. Show was at Leeds, where she was placed fourth in Not Separately Classified. Her first major win was at Blackpool Ch. Show when she won a first, also in the Not Separately Classified classes (the judge then was Mrs Josephine Creasy). What pleased the Osbornes more than anything was that the critique mentioned her as a Beardie; rather than as 'that grey dog'. Bluebelle was mated to Westernisles Brad of Bothkennar (owner Miss Gilchrist) but only one of that litter reached the show ring, winning first prizes before he was sent to Sweden where he became Swedish and Nordic International Ch. Bracken Boy from Osmart.

Mrs Catherine Parker (née Osborne) owns the best-known dog from the Osmart Kennels, Ch. Osmart Bonnie Blue Braid (Ch. Bravo of Bothkennar – Ch. Blue Bonnie of Bothkennar). He in his turn has sired eight Champions to date, and many C.C. winners: to name a few, Ch. Nigella Black Tango, Ch. Benedict Morning List, Ch. Brambledale Balthazaar, Ch. Willowmead Juno of Tambora. Blue Braid was a very dominant sire, and it is so easy to pick out his offspring, even when he was mated to bitches that do not come from the Osmart lines. Such a marked likeness to his famous sire is Mr and Mrs Jackson's Ch. Banacek Moonlight Blue, and this dog seems to get even more like him as he matures.

Mrs Trudi Wheeler, with the Cannamoor prefix, made up her first Champions in 1963, Ch. Cannamoor Brighde (Swalehall John Scrope – Brasenose Annabelle) shortly after her litter-sister Ch. Cannamoor Bonnie had also won her title. Both Bonnie and Brighde were born-black, and changed to grey later in life. Trudi mated Ch. Cannamoor

Brighde to Ch. Bravo of Bothkennar, and from the litter she picked out Cannamoor Carlotta to run on; Carlotta was brown and Mrs Wheeler was the first to experiment with a brown-to-brown mating, when she used Ch. Wishanger Cairnbahn as the stud dog. From that litter she kept Cannamoor Corn Marigold (brown) and mated her to her sire, the brown Ch. Wishanger Cairnbahn, so producing two generations of in-bred brown-to-brown.

Miss Mary Partridge owner of the Wishanger Kennels was given her first Bearded Collie dog, Ch. Wishanger Barley of Bothkennar, by her parents (as a prize for gaining her G.C.E. examination). Her first bitch she bought from Mr Keith Hicks, an early breeder, and named it Wishanger Jessica of Multan (Britt of Bothkennar ex Jennifer of Multan). Jessica was mated to Ch. Wishanger Barley of Bothkennar, and the litter produced the bitches Wishanger Wysteria, retained by Mary, and Wishanger Wychita, sold to Mrs Banks of the Gayfield Kennels. Wysteria was mated several times, and her name can be found in many of the breed pedigrees, having several Champions in her descendants. The second bitch to join the Wishanger

Left: Mrs Catherine Parker's Ch. Osmart Bonnie Blue Braid. *Centre*: Ch. Osmart Black Pearl. *Right*: Ch. Bravo of Bothkennar, owned by Mr and Mrs Osborne.

kennels was Ch. Willowmead my Honey, bought from Miss Suzanne Moorhouse, who bred her. The mating of Ch. Barley of Bothkennar to Ch. Willowmead my Honey produced the well-known bitch Ch. Wishanger Winter Harvest in their first litter; in the second litter was Wishanger Cuillin, Wishanger Clover Honey, and the famous Ch.

Lynne Evans' Ch. Brambledale Balthazar and his daughter Brambledale Black Rose.

Brambledale Balzac, Brambledale Baltaz and Brambledale Balika (all showing a very strong resemblance to their sire and grand-sire).

Wishanger Cairnbahn. So many top-quality and winning Beardies have descended from the handsome reddish-fawn Cairnbahn; he is a dog who attracted attention whenever he entered the show ring, with a wonderful out-going temperament, happy disposition, and profuse dark brown coat. This is the dog that I personally think has thrown his like for generation after generation when mated to so many different bitches.

One bitch in particular who was the image of her sire was Mrs Jackie Tidmarsh's Ch. Edelweiss of Tambora; her dam was Burdock of Tambora. Another in that same litter was Mrs Carol Walkden-Sturgeon's Alyshan Glengarry of Tambora; he won two C.C.s but never gained his title.

Mr and Mrs Jackson's Ch. Banacek Moonlight Blue (Ch. Osmart Bonnie Blue Braid ex Moonlight Mile of Kintop at Banacek).

Ch. Pepperland Lyric John at Potterdale has won 30 C.C.s, several Reserve C.C.s, Reserve B.I.S. All Breeds, and two Working Groups, and was also the Tambora Points Trophy winner for 1977, 1978, and 1979 (a trophy donated by the Bearded Collie Club for the top points winner for the year). He was also top stud dog for three consecutive years, 1981, 1982, and 1983. It certainly aroused interest when he entered the show ring in his heyday. He was bred by Leslie Samuels out of her bitch Pepperland Pandemonium and sired by Justine Warren's Wishanger Buttertubs Pass by Quinbury. Janet and Mike Lewis bought him as a puppy and campaigned him throughout his career. He was every inch a champion with excellent outline, super coat, and handsome strong head – some thought him very similar in looks to his great grandsire, Ch. Wishanger Cairnbahn. Lyric John was always presented in the most superb condition, never out of coat and spotlessly clean.

Miss M. Partridge's Ch. Wishanger Cairnbahn.

I saw his sire Wishanger Buttertubs Pass by Quinbury (Tubs for short) when his breeder brought him to Justine Warren's home. She kept him and added Quinbury to his already registered name. He was a dark slate puppy, with hardly any white markings, and I understood there was just one other bitch in the litter. Later when he was about two years old, I boarded him in our kennels and I found him to be of superb temperament. His coat stayed dark slate, long and very straight, and of good texture. Although quite a nice dog he was not a world beater, and at that time no one would have guessed that he

Miss M. Partridge's Ch. Wishanger Barley of Bothkennar, Ch. Willowmead My Honey, and Jessica of Multan.

could have sired such an outstanding dog as Lyric John, in the litter to Pandemonium.

Mr and Mrs Lewis' guiding star then led them to choose their beautiful multi-winning C.C. bitch Ch. Tamevalley Easter Song at Potterdale from the litter bred by Maureen Reader sired by Lyric John, out of her bitch Ch. Dutch Bonnet of Willowmead. This mating took place two more times, but it was the first litter that produced the Lewis' Easter Song, who followed closely in her sire's footsteps winning B.O.B.s and Groups and becoming the bitch C.C. record holder. Easter Song was mated to Bryony Harcourt Brown's well known Ch. Orora's Frank, a dog with a similar winning record. He in his turn was Top Beardie, winning the Tambora Points Trophy for 1983. He was sired by Ch. Osmart Bonnie Blue Braid out of Ch. Mignonette of Willowmead at Orora. From this mating the two latest champions came, Ch. Potterdale Philosopher and Potterdale Patch of Blue.

Miss Suzanne Moorhouse of the Willowmead prefix, will go down in the history of dog breeders as the first breeder to win Challenge Certificates at Crufts for three years in succession with the same gorgeous bitch, her Ch. Willowmead Perfect Lady.

Miss Moorhouse owned her first Beardie when she was a child; it died in 1947, and it was not until 1955 that she bought her first show Beardie, which was eventually to become Ch. Willowmead Barberry of Bothkennar, from Mrs Willison; this was the litter-sister to Ch. Wishanger Barley of Bothkennar. From her first litter, sired by Britt of Bothkennar, the very handsome Will o' wisp of Willowmead was retained. For her second litter, Barberry was mated to Int. Ch. Bobby of Bothkennar, and produced Merry Maker of Willowmead, and Moonmaiden of Willowmead. Miss Moorhouse then mated half-brother to half-sister, and from this mating came the famous Ch. Willowmead my Honey. Moonmaiden of Willowmead was sold to a Mrs Pitt, a Cavalier breeder living in Scotland; when she found a suitable working sheepdog she mated Moonmaiden to him and Suzanne received two of the puppies. One was Sweetheart of Willowmead; the other was Gypsy of Willowmead, who lived to the grand old age of 18 years – he must have been the oldest known living Beardie before he died in 1976. Sweetheart was mated to Will o' wisp; this litter produced Ruaridh of Willowmead, who was the foundation dog of Mrs Diane Hale's Broadholme strain. Later Suzanne Moorhouse rescued Ch. Broadholme Cindy Sue of Willowmead's brother, Braelyn

Mr Mike Lewis's Ch. Pepperland Lyric John at Potterdale.

Ch. Tamevalley
Easter Song of
Potterdale (Lyric
John's daughter).

Ch. Potterdale
Prelude (Ch.
Potterdale
Philosopher ex Ch.
Tamevalley Easter
Song of Potterdale).

Broadholme Crofter, from being put down. Both these Broadholme
Beardies feature in nearly all the Willowmead breeding, and have
given invaluable blood lines to many breeders. Recent well-known

descendants from the original Willowmead, down through the Broad-holme strain, are Mr Charlie Corderoy's Ch. Black Magic of Willow-mead, 1978 Cruft's winner; Miss Maureen Reader's Ch. Dutch Bon-net of Willowmead; Miss Harcourt Brown's Ch. Mignonette of Willowmead at Orora; and Ch. Sunbrees Magic Moments of Willow-mead, who is owned by Mrs Barbara Iremonger. Mrs Iremonger was Mrs Willison's kennel maid at the Bothkennar Kennels for six years prior to 1963; she handled many of the Bothkennar dogs in the show ring as well as for Obedience. She piloted Ch. Bosky Glen of Both-kennar (litter-brother to Ch. Bravo of Bothkennar) to gain his Show Ch. title. His first C.C. was won at Birmingham City Ch. Show, then he was taken into the Obedience Ring and won Test B, losing just one point for a wide heel-work. Barbara found this rather amusing, as she had worked hard with him all day trying to encourage him to walk away from her side in the Beauty Ring. His second C.C. was won at the L.K.A., and his third was at Cruft's, where he also gained Best of Breed. All Barbara's present-day Beardies descend from Ch. Sunbrees Magic Moments of Willowmead; in all he won 6 C.C.s and 14 Reserve C.C.s; also, he was a most lovable dog with the true Beardie character.

Magic Moments was mated to Barbatus Aurelia and produced in the litter Southernisles Perilla, who Barbara kept and eventually mated to Ch. Black Magic of Willowmead. From this litter Barbara picked the handsome dog and sire of so many winning offspring, Ch. Sunbree Sorceror.

In 1963 I became interested in the breed, but it was not easy to trace breeders with litters as there were so few being bred. I heard of Mrs Banks, owner of the Gayfield Kennels, and paid her a visit. The Gayfield Beardies went to most of the Championship Shows, but unfortunately, although they won Challenge Certificates, she was never lucky enough to make one a Champion. Mr Banks had been associated with the breed all his life; they were called 'Smithfield Drovers' on the farm where he worked, and were trained to take fifty sheep to Rochester Market about five miles away, and then to return home on their own. The farmers did not like the fancy name of Bearded Collies.

Mrs Banks's first show bitch was bought from Miss Mary Par-tridge, Wishanger Wychita; she mated her to Mrs Wheeler's Canna-moor Bailie, and started off one line of the Gayfield strain. She also bought stock from the Bothkennar kennels, Blue Streak of Bothken-nar and Bristly of Bothkennar; from these she bred Gayfield Wan-derer's Dream and Gayfield Rough Branches. I bought Gayfield Moonlight from her and showed her, though with only a little success.

I then heard that Miss Morris, of Binfield, Berkshire, had a litter

Miss Maureen Reader's Ch. Dutch Bonnet of Willowmead (Ch. Osmart Bonnie Blue Braid ex Breckdale Pretty Maid).

Mrs Barbara Iremonger's Ch. Sunbrees Magic Moments of Willowmead.

from the dark-slate dog Ch. Bosky Glen of Bothkennar, out of her own Martha Scrope of Swalehall; I bought Ch. Beagold Ella, a well marked dark-slate bitch, who was my foundation for the dark-slate and black breeding that I intended to follow. Soon after I bought Ella, Miss Jennifer Cooke bought the other bitch in the litter and took another route to the top, when she made her Obedience Ch. Scapa, the first Obedience Ch. in the breed to be invited to compete in Cruft's Obedience. 'Scapafield' then became Miss Cooke's prefix. Jennie Cooke, now Jennie Wiggins, became more interested in showing, and bought Ch. Osmart Black Lorraine from the Osmart Kennels. She started breeding several nice dogs and bitches, so the Scapafield prefix was seen on several C.C. winning Beardies.

I bred Ch. Beagold Ella to Ch. Wishanger Cairnbahn, and I was so pleased to see in the litter a born-black-and-white puppy that I could see would stay that colour, that I kept Beagold Buzz. Several generations later, with the black-and-white strong in the line, the dogs and bitches that I have exported have gained their titles in New Zealand, Canada, Holland, the States, Denmark, Germany and even Poland.

Mrs Tove Olsen's Eng. Int. Norw. Swed. Fin. Ch. Beagold David Blue (sire) and *right* Norw. and Swed. Ch. Beagold Nikki Nort (son).

I found the black and white colouring, that stayed black, very attractive, and continued to breed carefully so as to retain the darkest black puppy in each litter, to keep the colour in the breeding for the next generation (as mentioned in chapter 8). Beagold Porter Harvey continued producing the gorgeous strong black and white puppies in Denmark, especially when mated to Danish Ch. Osmart Black Buccaneer's daughters and granddaughters. In fact when I judged in Denmark in 1984 I was delighted to see the outstanding offspring from that combination. One dog in particular who is carrying on super colour and type is Suzanne Anderson's Danish Ch. Østermarks Chieftain.

Towards the end of the '60s, registrations had risen sharply, and with extra C.C.s on offer, there were more opportunities of making up a Champion. Mrs Vera Cooke was regularly exhibiting her dog Bredon Goblin (Ch. Wishanger Cairnbahn ex Bredon Mist), but it was not until 1970 that he gained his title (tragically dying shortly afterwards).

Mrs Betty Foster owns the Bredon prefix, and has been breeding for many years; her interests lie mainly in the Working and Obedience side, with beauty showings as a sideline. Her dog Wishanger Wild Hyacinth was the sire of the first Bearded Collie dog that I bought from Mrs Janet Martineau; Jayemji Derhue was out of her Obedience winning bitch Jayemji Doona. I did a little Obedience with Derhue and found him to be a keen and willing worker. He won B.O.B. at Leeds Ch. Show in 1969 but that was before C.C.s were on offer there. His next C.C. and B.O.B. was won at the W.E.L.K.S.; later he won the Reserve C.C. His main claim to fame was as the Gold Leaf cigarette advertising dog in 1969.

Miss Shirley Holme's Ch. Edenborough Blue Bracken, winner of 39 C.C.s up to mid-1979.

Mr and Mrs Roy Winwood bred Rowdina Grey Fella and Ch. Rowdina Rustler (Ch. Bracken Boy of Bothkennar ex Wishanger Crabtree). Rustler was sold to Mrs Mary Mathieson as a young dog, and she soon made him up to a Champion. He had a tragic end to his life when he panicked in a particularly bad storm and ran off for several weeks; when Mrs Mathieson eventually found him, he was in a very bad state, and not long afterwards, he had to be put down to prevent his suffering further.

Rowdina Grey Fella will go down in history as the sire of Shirley Holme's world famous Ch. Edenborough Blue Bracken, who is sadly no longer with us. He had a career that put him amongst the greatest; he won 39 C.C.s (an all-time record), three Best in Show wins at Championship Shows, five Best in Working Group, numerous Best in Show at Open Shows, and many other wins, even when he became a Veteran. He features strongly in so many pedigrees of present day Champions, that I can mention only a few; Ch. Edenborough Kara Kara; Ch. Edenborough Sweet Lady, owned by Beverly Cuddy, and who in her turn produced Champions; English and Canadian Ch. Edenborough Grey Shadow; Ch. Edenborough Amazing Grace; and the handsome black and white puppy that I bought from her in 1974, who later became Ch. Edenborough Star Turn at Beagold and who was winner of 16 Challenge Certificates, many Reserve C.C.s, two Reserve in the Working Group, and Winner of the Group. In his turn he has sired many Champions here and abroad, most famous amongst them being English, International, Norwegian, Swedish and Finnish Ch. Beagold David Blue, now owned and campaigned in Scandinavia by Mrs. Tove Olsen of Norway.

Star Turn's dam was Davealex Dawn Reign, who was bred by Jean and Derek Stopforth. Their Davealex strain has been well known for many years; one particular litter that caused quite a sensation in the breed was the first from Marilanz Amber Gleam (Ch. Wishanger Cairnbahn ex Broadholme Anne Marie) and Ch. Cala Sona Westernisles Loch Aber (Alastair of Willowmead ex Westernisles Wishanger Beechmast). Amber Gleam was another that closely resembled his sire, Ch. Wishanger Cairnbahn, and was owned at that time by Miss Harcourt Brown. His litter to Loch Aber was one of those never-to-be repeated lucky chances, providing seven C.C. winners in the one litter. Two of those made up to Champions (our Ch. Davealex Royle Baron and Mrs Tine Leonard's Ch. Davealex Royle Brigadier – who also had another claim to fame by being one of the grandsires of Ch. Pepperland Lyric John at Potterdale). The Stopforths kept Davealex Gorgeous Gussie; Mrs Foxcroft owned Davealex Royle Amber; Mrs Wolsey owned Davealex Royle Kinross; and Mrs Moira Morrison (of America) owned American and Canadian Ch. Davealex Larky

McRory. At the time of writing I still have Baron who has reached the magnificent age of 15 years, and the Stopforth's have Gorgeous Gussie. I do not know if the others are still alive. I have always loved that line and at the Beagold Kennels we have kept the strain going. We have Baron; Glynis Chambers has his son Beagold Fortune Beck and allows us to use him whenever we wish, we also have Fortune Beck's son Beagold Royal Fortune, and his daughter Beagold Royal Mist. Also we were lucky enough to purchase Blumberg Tapestry at Beagold (Ch. Edenborough Blue Bracken ex Davealex Highland Abbe), who is a younger sister of Baron. We are able to keep this bloodline well established in these kennels.

Ch. Edenborough Star Turn at Beagold when he won the Working Group at Bath Ch. Show in 1978.

Another well-known breeder who has made up Champions and produced consistently winning stock is Mrs Jacky James, of the Charncroft prefix. Ch. Charncroft Cassandra and Coraline she still owns, but Ch. Charncroft Corinth is owned by Mrs Pollard, and Charncroft Crusader was owned by Mrs Phyl Bailey. Crusader had the distinction of winning the C.C., B.O.B., then Working Group, and then Best in Show at the Scottish Ch. Show. Mrs Collins made up her bitch, Ch. Charncroft Country Maid; Miss Pat Jones owned Ch. Charncroft Cavalcade; Mr and Mrs Randall owned Charncroft

Country Lass at Kimrand, who was mated to their Ch. Kimrand Simon (Ch. Edenborough Star Turn at Beagold ex Kimrand Summer Dawn) and produced the two Champions Ch. Kimrand Star Gazer and Ch. Kimrand Saul.

1975–76 Miss Harcourt Brown won top Beardie with her gorgeous Ch. Mignonette of Willowmead at Orora; she continued winning top honours and crowned it by going B.O.B. at Crufts in 1976. The Orora Kennels have produced such quality Champions as Ch. Orora's Sugar Bush, Ch. Orora's Blue Basil, Ch. Orora's Huckleberry, Ch. Orora's Impetuosity, and Ch. Orora's Frank.

In Scotland, Major and Mrs Logan owned Glengorm Auld Clootie (Westernisles Wishanger Rough Grass ex Westernisles Loch Eport) and were very proud to announce that on 25 June 1978 Clootie became the first Scottish-owned Bearded Collie to win one hundred red cards.

Mr and Mrs Stopforth's Ch. Davealex Blaze Away at Osmart and Ch. Cala Sona Westernisles Loch Aber.

In 1963 Mrs Willison wrote in the *Dog World* Breed Notes that 'Miss Lynne Evans is having a good run of success with her young dog Brett, Heathermead Handsome' (Ch. Benjie of Bothkennar ex Beehoney of Bothkennar). Now, years later, American and Canadian Ch. Brambledale Blue Bonnet C.D. was the top-winning Beardie in America, with 70 B.O.B. wins to her credit. Bonnet is owned by Mr and Mrs Robert Lachman, but was bred by Miss Lynne Evans who owns the Brambledale prefix.

In Canada, Mrs Barbara Blake's Canadian Ch. Brambledale Boz was also doing his best to boost the Canadian Beardie population. Before he was sold to Canada, he won his Junior Warrant and a Res. C.C. over here. Lynne's Ch. Brambledale Balthazaar (Ch. Osmart Bonnie Blue Braid ex Brambledale Heathermead Moonlight) was the sire of Tine Batty's Blumberg De Roos Erasmus (now owned by Miss Andy Barker). He was mated to Chloe of Blumberg, and produced the exciting winning bitch Blumberg Hadriana of Potterdale. Mr and Mrs Appleby's Ch. Blumberg Diotima Steel was also sired by Ch. Brambledale Balthazaar, out of Davealex Highland Abbe, and she was litter-sister to Erasmus, two well-known winning Beardies.

The list of Junior Warrant winners grows longer at every show; there was a time – not so long ago – when it was much more difficult to gain the necessary 25 points needed to win a 'Junior Warrant'. Three points can be obtained only with a first win at a Championship Show, and one point in breed classes at an Open Show; there were so few classes for the breed at Open Shows, and Beardies had to be entered in the Variety classes. Tickets were on offer at very few shows after 1959, as there were only 65 Registrations for the breed at the Kennel Club that year. By 1967 they had risen to 163, and so more shows provided tickets. In 1984, C.C.s are on offer at every Championship Show that classifies Bearded Collies, plus three sets for the Breed Clubs. It is not long since the first Beardie was exported and made up to a Champion; now we have news daily of overseas Beardies gaining their titles, and winning in the Working Groups, with one or two even getting to win Best in Show at all Breed Shows.

The States have *Working Dog* magazine which gives monthly reports of 'Top-Producers' – they have made a survey of the dog who sires the most winning progeny, and he is the star of the month. They also publish the top dogs for the year. Although the Beardie was only recognised in America in early 1977, the breed was well established long before that date, and on gaining recognition they were all off like shots, with Champions being made up left and right; no doubt things will settle down before long, as competition gets keener.

There are also well-established Bearded Collie Clubs in many countries throughout the world; the Beardie has even reached Poland, where Frau Altmann made up her dog to Europa Sieger (Best of Breed winner) Int. Champion and Polish Ch. Beagold Errin. Now we have sent the first Bearded Collie to Greece, where we hope Beagold Black Jack will soon be campaigned and made up to a Champion.

Mrs Barbara Blake was the first registered Bearded Collie Kennels in Canada; her import from Mrs Nancy Scott, Canadian, Bermudan

Pat Jones' Ch. Wellknowe Shepherd Boy is the first English Champion sired by Shirly Holmes' Aust. Imp. Ardanne Kilmartin, out of Edenborough Blue Misty.

and American Ch. Willowferry Victor, with his 170 Best of Breed wins must have made the record in Canada. He now has 25 Champion descendants, most of the stock from the Colbara Kennels descend from Victor and her other import Brambledale Boz, who was sold to Mrs Blake by Miss Lynne Evans of the Brambledale Kennels, after he had won his Junior Warrant in Great Britain. Miss Carol Gold is a regular breeder and exhibitor in Canada, and has done so much to get the breed recognised by the ordinary show-going public. Her Ch. Raggmop Gaelin Image, and Ch. Wishanger Marsh Pimpernel, were well-known winners.

Since the breed was recognised in America a whole flock of Champions have gained their titles, and many new Beardie breeders have arrived on the scene. Two more Beardies went to the States in 1962, exported by Mrs Wheeler (Cannamoor) and Mrs Willison (Bothkennar). Dr and Mrs Levy took several Beardies back to the States with them, and the litter planned between Cannamoor Glen Canach and Cannamoor Carndoonagh would be the first recorded Bearded Collie litter known in the States. The early breeders had really to struggle for recognition against enormous odds, and spent much time, money and effort for the benefit of their dogs. Notable kennels from the first were of course the Levy's Heathglen; Mr and Mrs Morrison's Cauldbrae Kennels; the Dunwich Kennels, owned by Dr and Mrs Thomas

Davies; the Dolans and their Glen Eire Beardies; the Parson family's Braemoor Beardies; Mrs Joan Surber's Wyndcliff Kennels. Mrs Surber became so engrossed with the breed that she published a most interesting and popular magazine *The Bearded Collie*. There must have been others who supported the names I have mentioned. The dedication and hard work paid off, and the Bearded Collie is now recognised in the States.

The situation on the Continent is much the same. Some of the first Beardies ever to be seen in Finland were the two sent by Mrs Willison to Mrs Sundstrom; Int. Ch. Ambassador of Bothkennar and Ch. Beeflower of Bothkennar. I was invited to judge in Finland in 1978, and was able to see for myself what strides they have made, despite so many difficulties. The one advantage of breeding in that country is the space, miles and miles of forests and woodlands where the dogs can be exercised to their hearts' content.

In 1960, Bencha of Bothkennar was sent to Italy; Bencha was the half-brother of Miss Lynne Evans's Ch. Heathermead Handsome, and these two dogs are the only two sons of the well-known Benji of Bothkennar to be used at stud. Mrs Kurzbein, of the Elsternhoh prefix in Switzerland, used Bencha of Bothkennar on her Beauty's Bairn of Bothkennar, bought from Mrs Willison a couple of years previously, and from the litter she kept for breeding and showing Andra von der Elsternhoh; shortly after Andra was mated to Int. Nat. Champion Blue Jacket of Bothkennar (Ch. Bravo of Bothkennar ex Ch. Blue Bonnie of Bothkennar) and Mrs Kurzbein kept Doret von der Elsternhoh. She was very pleased to have retained the bitch and not lost the line, as during a very bad storm Andra was killed by lightning. Mrs Kurzbein was the top breeder in Switzerland, and used to make an annual visit to Cruft's; on one of her visits she bought Hyfield Myridon (Ch. Wishanger Cairnbahn ex Hyfield Kirtel) and when he was mated to Doret the two well-known dogs Int. Nat. Ch. Fant von der Elsternhoh, and litter brother Swiss Ch. Hylas von der Elsternhoh were born.

The first Beardie to go to Holland, about twenty years ago (sent by Miss Suzanne Moorhouse), was Lone Charm of Willowmead. Mrs Lensvelt then bought Windmill Hill Wayfarer from the breeder Captain Owen. Not long after, the Dutch Beardie owners formed their own Club. For several years Mrs Annie Schneider Louter campaigned her Bearded Collies in Holland. Best-known of her kennel were Int. Ch. Elderberry of Tambora, and Ch. Oliver Black of Tambora. She has travelled to many countries exhibiting her Warwinckel stock.

We sold Int. Ch. Dutch Ch. Lux. Ch. Eurocup winner 1979, 1980, 1981 Beagold Bruin Scott to Ben and Marj Scholte way back in 1976;

Marie and Joseph Volkers, owners of the Babbacombe Bearded Collies. Marie is with Beagold Blizzard, and Joseph is with the dark brown Beagold Wayward Lad. They have taken their dogs to many of the Continental Ch. Shows, and have won constantly.

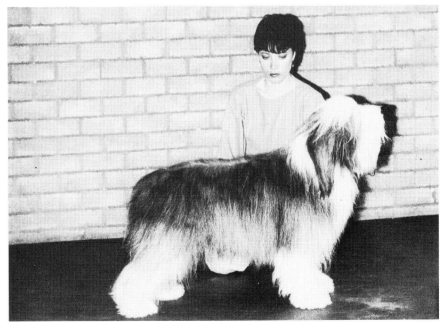

they campaigned him extensively throughout Europe and he was Dog of the Year All Breeds in 1981, which was a great achievement for a Bearded Collie as none had ever reached such heights before. Bruin Scott was sired by Ch. Edenborough Star Turn at Beagold out of Beagold Penny Royal. Another top winner that came to Holland from these kennels was Int. Ch. Beagold Black Moses owned and campaigned by Marie Volkers. Moses was sired by Am. Ch. Kimrand Drummer Boy at Beagold out of Beagold Hanna N'Vier.

Mrs Barbro Finkelstein of the Bellbreed Kennels in Sweden started with the foundation bitch Bifrost Beau Shaggie, daughter of Int. Nord. Champion Rowdina Main Attraction. Since then she has also imported from England; Bluebell from Osmart, Briaridge Black Ace, and Glenwhin Kinair Loch. All have won their titles, and have proved a firm foundation on which the Bellbreed Beardie strain was built. Mr Bowman of the Happy Dog Beardies bought Wishanger Rough Gale (Alastair of Willowmead ex Ch. Wishanger Winter Harvest) to join Wishanger Winterberry who was bought from Miss Partridge in 1960.

Another Swedish breeder who has been very interested in the breed for some time is Mrs Olson, who bought Jayemji Cluni (Ch. Wishanger Cairnbahn ex Merrymaker of Willowmead) from Mrs Janet Martineau, and Bracken Boy from Osmart from Mr and Mrs Osborne. These famous kennels now have many Champions, and produce top quality stock from many imports from this country.

Mrs Helga Pederson of the Vigsbjerg Kennels, Denmark, owns the top stud and best-known winning dog, Ch. Osmart Black Buccaneer (Broadholme Buccaneer ex Ch. Osmart Bonnie Black Pearl); he could be considered the foundation dog upon which the subsequent history of the Beardie rests in Denmark. When I judged in Denmark in 1977, I could see the strong resemblance to Buckaneer in so many of the exhibits; nearly all the dogs and bitches at that show had him somewhere in their pedigrees. One or two breeders foresaw the danger of arriving at a situation where there were no bloodlines that did not descend from the one dog and imported other Beardies. Mrs Hindesgaul bought Beagold Porter Harvey from us, and he was used extensively at stud to many of the Black Buckaneer offspring. The bloodlines obviously tied in well together; imagine my delight when I was confronted with so many outstanding black and white super-quality Beardies at the Championship Show in 1984 in Denmark. Later I found them mainly descendants of those two dogs. Temperament, construction, and coat texture were excellent – although it was generally thought that blacks had soft coat, it was not so in these Beardies.

Space does not allow me to mention all the Champions that have been made up in recent years. What I have tried to do is mention the early ones who have set the pattern for the modern quality dogs and bitches.

Finally, while saluting the formidable list of Breeders and their Champions, I do not forget the dedicated exhibitors who have yet to reach the top. There are many also who do not have ambitions to make up Champions or to shine in the show ring, and who continue to breed for Obedience, for Working, or just to produce loving companion dogs.

It is now twenty-one years since I owned my first Bearded Collie. So many marvellous characters have given me love, affection and companionship; many are dead and gone a long time ago but the memories remain. As the time draws near when another beloved pet reaches the end my heart breaks again. But there is never a time when I do not gather around me the ones that are left, and thank goodness there will be many more years when I shall get joy and pleasure from owning this marvellous breed.

There are many other breeders who gain as much pleasure from their Beardies and organise their lives so that it includes those hairy 'monsters'. Lynne Evans of the Brambledale prefix has owned and loved Beardies longer than I have. She wrote an article for the *Beardie News* and has given me permission to include it here for other people's pleasure:

The Sinners by Lynne Evans

In the gloom at the top of the orchard a small grey figure stands hunched in the rain. Its dejected attitude exudes such misery and isolation that even the stoniest heart must bleed. From the bottom of the steps I call again, as I have called a dozen times in the last hour, waiting for the familiar response of the slim silver form leaping gaily down the steep slope, eyes shining, tail flying to greet me with a Beardie smile and dance. But not now. Nothing.

The figure under the trees remains unmoved as I turn back into the house, closing the door quickly to preserve the pleasant fug in the Beardie room where eleven contented after-dinner bodies luxuriate in the rosy glow of an infra-red lamp. Not one gives a thought to the waif in the mist. Her fat black brother beams smugly from between his two grandmothers. Even her mother dreams happily of the day's events, her feet twitching as she relives the familiar excitement of the forest.

No one cares that Dolly was SCOLDED this afternoon and will never recover. It has been raining since last June. It has, in fact, been raining for all of Dolly's life, since she was only born in October. Which is unfortunate because Dolly doesn't like the rain.

Several of the Beardies share her aversion, though they all manage to overcome it for an hour or two each morning when we take our daily walk in the forest. Once that is over, though, the rain-haters take to their beds and rumour has it that on very wet days some of them will resist the call of nature for twenty-four hours rather than brave the dripping orchard.

Puppies, however, cannot be allowed to attempt such feats of endurance and a reluctant Dolly must be chivvied up the steps to join a cheerful band of wet footed relations who have enormous fun pushing each other into the water-logged ditch.

And so it was this afternoon. Only today I didn't chivvy quite fast enough and the result was a pool on the floor. Now you might think that in a doggy household a puddle here or there would pass unnoticed, and so it might were it not for the fastidious nature of the adult Beardies who regard such accidents with the deepest hor-ror and insist that any room so dampened must be instantly evacu-ated, disinfected, dried and aired before they can bring themselves to enter it again.

In deference to their feelings, puppies are restricted to their own room and banned from the dog-room until old enough to keep the rules. Dolly and brother James have only recently been promoted to adult status and to their elders and betters Dolly's lapse was an unforgivable breach of privilege. Even at the other end of the room elderly matrons lept to their feet in horror and scrambled on to tables and benches in exaggerated anticipation of a rising water-level. The air was heavy with disapproval which was not lost on Dolly and a single exclamation from me was enough to send her scuttling out of the door and up the orchard steps to take refuge among the trees at the top. And there she stayed.

And she's still there.

Silly little thing. She can come in if she wants to. And she needn't think that I'm going up there to coax her down now that I've got my slippers on and hung my wet coat up to dry. I'll just open the door to see if she's there. She isn't, and it's so dark and misty now that I can only just make out the insubstantial shape under the trees. A sad little presence dripping in the darkness with a misery that reaches out to take me in an instant back to a day more than twenty-five years ago when another forlorn figure stood under an apple tree in a garden far away. Nothing insubstantial about this one though. A fat little girl with corkscrew curls sticking to round cheeks wet with angry tears. 'I won't go in – not EVER! I'll just stay here all night and I'll die and THEN they'll be sorry.' The reason is forgotten but the emotion returns as fresh as ever and I smile as I climb the slippery steps to the sodden pup in the darkness. Water seeps through my slippers as I scoop her up in my arms for a cuddle. 'Don't die, Dolly – we'd be EVER so sorry.'

KENNEL CLUB REGISTRATIONS

It is very interesting to note the number of Beardies registered at The Kennel Club, from the very first, Mrs Willison's Jennie of Bothkennar, registered in 1948. Bailie of Bothkennar was registered in 1949. From then on the registrations rose very slightly, until a big jump in 1956 and 1957; there were falls in 1958 and 1961. The increase in numbers then remained steady.

1948	1	1957	70	1966	134	1975	★ 677
1949	1	1958	41	1967	163	1976	★ 402
1950	7	1959	65	1968	244	1977	★ 373
1951	3	1960	77	1969	276	1978	★ 757
1952	7	1961	48	1970	308	1979	★1082
1953	12	1962	93	1971	444	1980	★1345
1954	19	1963	59	1972	565	1981	★1179
1955	18	1964	121	1973	661	1982	★1179
1956	56	1965	148	1974	651	1983	★1371

★In 1975, The Kennel Club stopped including all dogs in a breed on the same Register and divided the Register into Basic and Active. Only Active figures are published.

THE BEARDED COLLIE CLUB

The Bearded Collie Club as we know it was founded in 1955; Miss Doris Lowe was the Treasurer and Secretary, and organised the first Club Show in 1959. The Beardies were then so few on the ground that Rough and Smooth Collies were invited to enter the classes put on for them.

As more people became interested in the Breed, and Registrations increased, the Club was able to give the Breed eleven classes at the Show held in 1966, at the St Luke's Church Hall in Shepherd's Bush. The Puppy and Junior Classes in both sexes were fairly well filled but the Open Dog Class had one entry and four absentees. The one dog, Miss Lynne Evans's Ch. Heathermead Handsome beat the bitch for Best Opposite Sex. The Bitch winner, Nick Broadbridge's Bredon Whisper won Limit and Open. I remember the St Luke's Hall as a small place, with none of the facilities to make the show a great success. But the wonderful friendly atmosphere and welcome from the Bearded Collie owners was warm and sociable. Judge for the Beardies at that show was Mrs Trudi Wheeler; the six Rough Collie Classes were judged by Mrs Iris Coombe.

The next Show held at the same venue was judged by Miss Michele Taffe (Heathermead, and now Mrs Michele James). This was in 1967 and the 14 Classes had an average of 8 per class. Looking through the catalogue, I see that Wishanger River Humber was a Puppy, Osmart Bonnie Blue Braid was in Junior, and Ch. Wishanger Cairnbahn was being shown in Open Dog. The beautiful silver-grey bitch Glendonald Silver Braid owned by Mrs Michel at her first venture into the show ring won Puppy, Junior, Novice and Graduate and then Best in Show.

We moved from St Luke's Hall to The Parkside Hall, Ampthill, in Bedfordshire for our show in 1970. Miss Suzanne Moorhouse was the popular judge who drew the magnificent entry of 185, with 98 Exhibits. Mrs Winwood won three classes with her dog Rowdina Happy Sam; he was then made Best Puppy in Show. I was very pleased to win the Graduate Class that had 14 entries with my black and white dog Beagold Buzz. Open Dog class was won by Miss Catherine Osborne's now-Ch. Osmart Bonnie Blue Braid, who also won Best in Show. Winner of Graduate Bitch was Mrs Warren's Wishanger Misty Hollow, who later became a Champion. The winner of Limit and Open Bitch was also Best Opposite Sex winner, the lovely bitch Ch. Wishanger Waterfall owned by Miss Pat Gilpin, (now Mrs Fisk). Waterfall won 6 Challenge Certificates in all, became Bitch of the Year, winning the Tambora Points Trophy for 1970, and won a Reserve C.C. at Cruft's at the age of 9 years.

In 1971, the Club moved to the Borough Hall, Stafford, to hold the first Open Show for the year. Mr Roy Winwood officiated, and was very pleased to receive 199 entries. Many more new members entered their dogs and bitches, and the Open Dog class had such well known dogs as Braelyn Broadholme Crofter, Ch. Osmart Bonnie Blue Braid, Ch. Wishanger Cairnbahn, and Rowdina Grey Fella. There were also the two dogs Brambledale Balthazaar and Sunbrees Magic Moments of Willowmead before they became Champions, and Marilanz Amber Gleam, then owned by the Stopforths. The Open Bitch class had Ch. Marilanz Anneliese (litter sister to Amber Gleam) Ch. Wishanger Waterfall, Ch. Broadholme Adorable, and Ch. Osmart Bonnie Black Pearl. In October that year the Bearded Collie Club held a second show, this time on my doorstep in Hitchin. I was honoured to be asked to judge. This was a 20-Class Open Show and I received the magnificent entry of 216, with 103 exhibitors. My Best in Show winner was Mrs Barbara Iremonger's Sunbrees Magic Moments of Willowmead, before he became a Champion. My best bitch was Mr and Mrs Stopforth's Davealex Gorgeous Gussie. Best Puppy was Mr and Mrs Osborne's Osmart She's Blue Beth.

The First Club Championship Show took place on 25 March 1972. Mrs Diane Hale (Broadholme) had the honour of officiating. This was held in Staffordshire and we were given 20 classes. An excellent entry of 208, with many Champions, attended. The first winner in Open Dog was Miss Osborne's Ch. Osmart Bonnie Blue Braid; and the first winner in Open Bitch was Miss Suzanne Moorhouse's Ch. Willowmead Juno of Tambora (Ch. Osmart Bonnie Blue Braid ex Ch. Edelwiess of Tambora).

The Club then began to cater regularly for the widespread membership, holding regular shows in the North and South, and the Championship Shows in the Midlands. Usually, specialist judges were asked to officiate, but the first all-rounder judge was Miss Jean Lanning, who drew an entry of 295 when she judged in 1973. Her Best in Show winner was Miss Shirley Holme's Ch. Edenborough Blue Bracken. The next all-rounder to Judge was Mr Tom Horner at the Slough Community venue. Best in Show winner then was Miss Shirley Holme's Ch. Edenborough Blue Bracken again. Reserve Best in Show was Capt and Mrs Warren's Barnleigh Damaris (Marksman of Sunbree ex Cannamoor Corndolly). I remember competing for the Reserve Best in Show with my Ch. Davealex Royle Baron against Barnleigh Damaris. Baron had mated Damaris the previous week, and as we took our Beardies around the ring with Damaris in front, Baron suddenly realised who we were following. I have never known him to move so fast! Soon after that win Barnleigh Damaris was taken back to the States by the Warrens, and then after winning the necessary points became an American Champion.

There was a great increase in the number of Beardies shown at Championship Shows at the end of the 1970s and in the early 1980s. However in 1983 and the first half of 1984 it seems to have slowed down for many reasons – one being that we have Challenge Certificates on offer at 36 Championship Shows, so that exhibitors can pick and choose shows with not too great a journey. Also after showing under a judge who has not liked your dog, there is no point in travelling miles at great expense only to be thrown out again. Most members like to attend Breed Club Shows, but here again there is no point in going to such a show knowing that the judge will not place your dog.

The Bearded Collie Club committee then decided to organise less formal get-togethers, and someone came up with the idea of calling them 'Bearded Collie Bounce-Ins'. The first was held at the Parkside Hall, Ampthill, Bedfordshire. A very interesting programme was arranged, which included a puppy walk, an Obedience demonstration given by Miss Morris's Tannochbrae (Scapa's brother), who loved to jump and delighted everyone with his skill. (No five-foot fence would deter him from escaping if he wished!).

The highlight of the programme was the parade of Champions. That was when the cameras were very busy, as the dogs and bitches in the parade were just names on pedigrees to some that were there. This was 1969 and many of the Champions and C.C. winners were at the retirement age then. Those that took part were Cannamoor Bailie, Merry Maid of Willowmead (C.C. winners), Ch. Cannamoor Brighde, Ch. Bravo of Bothkennar, Ch. Bosky Glen of Bothkennar, Ch. Cannamoor Fraukie, Ch. Heathermead Handsome, Ch. Wishanger Crabtree, Ch. Beagold Ella, Ch. Osmart Bonnie Blue Braid, Beardie Bell C.D. Ex., and the two most-publicised Beardies of the year, Miss Lynne Evans Brambledale Briar Rose, who had been featured in a television series, and my Jayemiji Derhue, who had been chosen from so many other dogs to advertise Players Gold Leaf cigarettes. (He was featured in all the National papers, and displayed on huge posters all over the country with his beautiful expression depicting *Trust*. There was Derhue looking trustfully up into the face of the male model holding a packet of Gold Leaf Cigarettes).

There have been many Bounce-Ins held since by various Branches, but that first was the best.

The membership of the original Bearded Collie Club became very large and unwieldy; there were so many members in large pockets dotted around the country with very little chance of travelling to the Shows or the one Bounce-In held by the Club each year, so it was decided to form Branches to cater for the different areas.

There was every sign that another Bearded Collie Club was needed, and as the 'centre' of the original Club (President, Chairman, Secretary and Treasurer) had moved from the South to the North, the proposed new Club was formed and called The Southern Counties Bearded Collie Club. The inaugural meeting was held in 1976, The next Bearded Collie Club to be formed was The Bearded Collie Club of Scotland. Now we have the fourth Club, The Eastern Bearded Collie Association, recognised by the Kennel Club in October 1984.

Miss Morris with Tannochbrae, who is showing his agility in Obedience.

Appendix 1

Table of Champions in the Breed – Dogs

Name of Dog	*Owner*	*Breeder*
Benjie of Bothkennar	Mrs Willison	Mrs Willison
Bravo of Bothkennar	Mr & Mrs Osborne	Mrs Willison
Boskie Glen of Bothkennar	Mr & Mrs Webberley	Mrs Willison
Bracken Boy of Bothkennar	Miss S. Holmes	Mrs Willison
Bobby of Bothkennar	Mrs Pickford	Mrs Willison
Wishanger Cairnbahn	Miss Partridge	Miss M. Partridge
Wishanger Cuillin	Miss Griffin	Miss M. Partridge
Heathermead Handsome	Miss Evans	Mrs James
Brambledale Balthazaar	Miss Evans	Miss Evans
Davealex Blaze Away at Osmart	Mr & Mrs Stopforth	Mr & Mrs Osborne
Davealex Royle Baron	Mrs Collis & Mr Cosme	Mr & Mrs Stopforth
Davealex Royle Brigadier	Mrs Batty	Mr & Mrs Stopforth
Osmart Black Barnacle from Penhallow	Mrs Pickford	Mr & Mrs Osborne
Osmart Bonnie Blue Braid	Mrs Ryan	Mr & Mrs Osborne
Padworth Duke	Mr & Mrs Nunly	Mr Prestidge
Rowdina Rustler	Mrs Mathieson	Mr Winwood
Sunbrees Magic Moments of Willowmead	Mrs B. Iremonger	Miss Moorhouse
Black Magic of Willowmead	Mr & Mrs Corderoy	Miss Moorhouse
Wishanger Barley of Bothkennar	Miss Partridge	Miss Partridge
Benedict Morning Mist	Mr J. Stanbridge	Mr C. Barker
Bancek Moonlight Blue	Mr & Mrs Jackson	Mr & Mrs Jackson
Bredon Goblin	Mrs Cooke	Mrs Foster
Charncroft Cassandra	Mr James	Mrs James
Charncroft Corinth	Mr & Mrs Pollard	Mrs James
Edenborough Blue Bracken	Miss Holmes	Miss Holmes
Edenborough Grey Shadow	Miss Holmes	Miss Holmes
Pepperland Lyric John at Potterdale	Mr & Mrs Lewis	Miss Samuels
Edenborough Brown Bracken	Miss Holmes	Miss Holmes
Sheldawyn Black Jet at Hajacen	Mrs Metcalf	Miss Todd
Orora's Blue Basil	Miss Harcourt Brown	Miss Harcourt Brown
Kimrand Simon	Mr & Mrs Randall	Mr & Mrs Randall
Edenborough Star Turn at Beagold	Mr Cosme & Mrs Collis	Miss Holmes
Kimrand Smokey Joe	Mr & Mrs Beauchamp	Mr & Mrs Randall
Zorisaan Chocolate Surprise at Kewella	Mrs Brooks	Mr & Mrs Bell
Orora's Frank	Miss Harcourt Brown	Miss Harcourt Brown
Grizlinda Morning Monarch at Akooshla	Mr & Mrs Hawkins	Mr & Mrs Dodds
Sunbree Sorcerer	Mr & Mrs Iremonger	Mr & Mrs Iremonger
Wellknowe Shepherd Boy	Miss Jones	Miss Jones
Charncroft Cavalcade	Miss Jones	Mrs James
Potterdale Philosopher	Mr & Mrs Lewis	Mr & Mrs Lewis
Potterdale Patch of Blue	Mr & Mrs Lewis	Mr & Mrs Lewis
Beagold David Blue	Mrs Collis & Mr Cosme	Mrs Collis & Mr Cosme

Name of Dog	*Owner*	*Breeder*
Willowmead Star Attraction	Mr & Mrs O'Brien	Miss Moorhouse
Kimrand Saul	Mr & Mrs Randall	Mr & Mrs Randall
Moonhills Gold Digger	Mrs B White	Mrs B White
Sunkap Adam	Mr & Mrs Young	Mr & Mrs Young
Deldrove Debonair of Padworth	Mr & Mrs Prestidge	Mrs Henning
Sunkap Bartholomew of Cregah	Mr & Mrs Kirk	Mr & Mrs Young
Orora's Impetuosity	Miss Harcourt Brown	Miss Harcourt Brown
Swinford Sky Rocket at Macmont	Mrs Richardson	Mrs Collins
Wellknowe Crofter	Miss P. Jones	Miss P. Jones

Table of Champions in the Breed – Bitches

Name of Bitch	*Owner*	*Breeder*
Beauty Queen of Bothkennar	Mrs Willison	Mrs Willison
Blue Bonnie of Bothkennar	Mr & Mrs Osborne	Mrs Willison
Bronze Penny of Bothkennar	Mrs Willison	Mr K. Hicks
Willowmead Barberry of Bothkennar	Miss Moorhouse	Mrs Willison
Beagold Ella	Mrs Collis	Miss Morris
Cannamoor Fraukie	Mrs Anderson	Mrs Anderson
Cannamoor Brighde	Mrs Wheeler	Mrs Wheeler
Cannamoor Bonnie	Mrs Wheeler	Mrs Wheeler
Osmart Bonnie Black Pearl	Mrs Osborne	Mrs Osborne
Cala Sona Westernisles Loch Aber.	Mr & Mrs Stopforth	Miss Gilchrist
Edelweiss of Tambora	Mrs Tidmarsh	Mrs Tidmarsh
Wishanger Winter Harvest	Miss Partridge	Miss Partridge
Wishanger Crab Tree	Mrs D. Winwood	Miss Partridge
Wishanger Waterfall	Miss Fisk	Mrs Broadbridge
Wishanger Misty Hollow	Mrs Warren	Miss Partridge
Willowmead Super Honey	Miss Moorhouse	Miss Moorhouse
Black Velvet of Willowmead	Miss Moorhouse	Miss Moorhouse
Willowmead Juno of Tambora	Miss Moorhouse	Mrs Tidmarsh
Sheldawyn Snowflake	Miss Todd	Miss Todd
Penhallows Pink Panther	Mr Maskell	Mrs Pickford
Osmart Black Pollyana	Mrs Osborne	Mrs Osborne
Mignonette of Willowmead at Orora	Miss Harcourt Brown	Miss Moorhouse
Broadholme Cindy Sue of Willowmead	Miss Moorhouse	Mrs Hale
Willowmead my Honey	Miss Partridge	Miss Moorhouse
Edenborough Kara Kara of Josanda	Mrs Pendlebury	Miss Holmes
Edenborough Sweet Lady	Miss Cuddy	Miss Holmes
Edenborough Amazing Grace	Miss Holmes	Miss Holmes
Charncroft Coralline	Mrs James	Mrs James
Chantala Wishanger Craggy Tor	Miss Donechy	Miss Partridge
Broadholme Adorable	Mrs Hale	Mrs Hale
Broadholme Bonnie Jean	Mrs Durrant	Mrs Hale
Andrake Black Diamond	Mr Diamond	Mrs Drake
Andrake Persephone	Mr Drake	Mr Drake
Chantala Corrie	Miss Donechy	Miss Donechy
Marilanz Anneleise	Mrs Benyon	Mrs Benyon
Nigella Black Tango	Mr & Mrs Meyrick	Mrs Osborne
Sheldawyn Blue Opal	Miss Todd	Miss Todd
Dutch Bonnet of Willowmead	Miss Maureen Reader	Miss Moorhouse
Orora's Sugar Bush	Miss Harcourt Brown	Miss Harcourt Brown
Charncroft Cassandra	Mrs James	Mrs James
Blumberg Hadriana at Potterdale	Mr & Mrs Lewis	Mrs Batty
Diotima Dream Baby	Mr & Mrs Appleby	Mr & Mrs Appleby
Blumberg Diotima Steel	Mr and Mrs Appleby	Mr & Mrs Batty

Name of Bitch	Owner	Breeder
Kimrand Carousel	Mr & Mrs Copus	Mr & Mrs Randall
Lordryn Lady Palastrina	Mr & Mrs Croot	Mr & Mrs Croot
Queen Arwen of Kenstaff	Miss Hannah	Mr & Mrs Osborne
Potterdale Prelude	Mr & Mrs Lewis	Mr & Mrs Lewis
Tamevalley Easter Song at Potterdale	Mr & Mrs Lewis	Miss Reader
Kilrenny Cherokee	Mr & Mrs Manning	L. Oakes
Willowmead Perfect Lady	Miss Moorhouse	Miss Moorhouse
Arranbourne Charisma	Mrs Prince	Mrs Prince
Kimrand Stargazer	Mr & Mrs Randall	Mr & Mrs Randall
Scapafield Light Raine	Mrs Troughton	Mrs Wiggins
Osmart Black Thorn of Moonhill	Mrs B. White	Mr & Mrs Osborne
Osmart Black Orraine	Mrs J. Wiggins	Mr & Mrs Osborne
Willowmead Summer Wine	Miss Wilding	Miss Moorhouse
Sunkap Chantilly	Mr & Mrs Young	Mr & Mrs Young
Sunkap Abbi	Mr & Mrs Young	Mr & Mrs Young
Dajue Copper Honey Bun	Mrs Emmet	Mrs Emmet
Bryole Peppers Pride	Mr Cross	Mr Cross
Shenendene Rustic Miss	Miss Kimber	Mr & Mrs Hall
Joclabar Annie's Girl	Mrs Cross	Mr & Mrs Diamond
Robdave Wild Affair	Mr & Mrs Forrest	Mr & Mrs Hinton
Orora's Sugar Plum of Hajacan	Mrs Metcalf	Miss Harcourt Brown
Dorvicson Society Belle	Mrs Jackson	Mrs Jackson

Champions in the Breed at Cruft's

In the early days it was not necessary to qualify for Cruft's, but it was every breeder's aim to take their dogs to that 'Greatest Show on Earth'. The entries for Cruft's then became so many that the Kennel Club brought in the qualifying rules. Cruft's 1971 published the first rules, by which it was quite easy to win qualifiers; each year further rules were made to cut down the numbers quite drastically. Most recently, a first win in Minor Puppy, Puppy, Junior, Post Graduate, Limit or Open classes is required to qualify.

C.C. winner and B.O.B.	C.C. winner (B.O.S.)
1959 Ch. Beauty Queen of Bothkennar	Britt of Bothkennar
1960 Ch. Wishanger Barley of Bothkennar	Ch. Willowmead Barberry of Bothkennar
1961 Ch. Benjie of Bothkennar	Ch. Willowmead My Honey
1962 Ch. Bravo of Bothkennar	Ch. Blue Bonnie of Bothkennar
1963 Ch. Benjie of Bothkennar	Ch. Bronze Penny of Bothkennar
1964 Ch. Benjie of Bothkennar	Wishanger Winter Harvest
1965 Bosky Glen of Bothkennar	Cannamoor Fraukie
1966 Ch. Wishanger Cairnbahn	Ch. Cannamoor Fraukie
1967 Ch. Broadholme Adorable	Ch. Bravo of Bothkennar
1968 Ch. Wishanger Crabtree	Yealand Conrad
1969 Ch. Bracken Boy of Bothkennar	Ch. Edelweiss of Tambora
1970 Chantala Corrie	Ch. Wishanger Cairnbahn
1971 Ch. Edelweiss of Tambora	Ch. Rowdina Rustler
1972 Ch. Osmart Bonnie Blue Braid	Ch. Wishanger Misty Hollow
1973 Ch. Edenborough Blue Bracken	Ch. Charncroft Cassandra
1974 Ch. Edenborough Blue Bracken	Wichnor Wild Cherry of Milltop
1975 Ch. Brambledale Balthazaar	Ch. Andrake Black Diamond

C.C. winner and B.O.B.	*C.C. winner (B.O.S.)*
1976 Ch. Mignonette of Willowmead at Orora	Ch. Davealex Royle Brigadier
1977 Ch. Penhallow Pink Panther	Ch. Edenborough Blue Bracken
1978 Ch. Black Magic of Willowmead	Ch. Willowmead Perfect Lady
1979 Ch. Pepperland Lyric John at Potterdale	Ch. Willowmead Perfect Lady
1980 Ch. Black Magic of Willowmead	Ch. Willowmead Perfect Lady
1981 Ch. Kimrand Stargazer	Ch. Pepperland Lyric John at Potterdale
1982 Ch. Willowmead Star Attraction	Ch. Blumberg Diotima Steel
1983 Ch. Tamevalley Easter Song at Potterdale	Ch. Kimrand Saul
1984 Ch. Zorisaan Chocolate Surprise at Kewella	Ch. Shenendene Rustic Miss
1985 Quinbury Stormdrifter at Runival CD ex.	Ch. Diotima Dream Baby

Ch. Benjie of Bothkennar is the only dog to have won a C.C. at Crufts three times.

Ch. Willowmead Perfect Lady is the only bitch to have won a C.C. at Crufts three times.

Mrs Jenny Osborne was the first Specialist Judge to give C.C.s at Crufts, in 1975.

The following Bearded Collies have won the Working Group at General Championship Shows under Kennel Club rules:
Ch. Andrake Persephone
Ch. Edenborough Blue Bracken★★
Charncroft Crusader★★
Ch. Mignonette of Willowmead at Orora
Ch. Robdave Wild Affair★
Ch. Pepperland Lyric John at Potterdale★
Ch. Edenborough Star Turn at Beagold
Ch. Kimrand Simon
Ch. Tamevalley Easter Song of Potterdale★
Ch. Osmart Black Thorn of Moonhill
Ch. Grizlinda Morning Monarch
Pure Magic of Willowmead
Ch. Orora's Impetuousity
Ch. Orora's Frank
Ch. Kimrand Smokey Joe
★★ Best in Show; ★ Reserve Best in Show

Appendix 2

The Bearded Collie Working Tests
It was decided in 1969 to compile Working Tests for Bearded Collies, so that the breed would not become just glamour-dogs which never attempt to use their intelligence. The dogs cannot be kept in pastoral occupation, so the Tests were compiled to keep their minds active and their bodies occupied.

Winners of the Senior Working Test Award
1969: Mrs Griffiths' Cannamoor Carn Roxie
1970: Miss Evans's Ch. Heathermead Handsome; Miss Gallatly's Brambledale Bess and Filabey Delicia; Mrs Griffiths' Rainbird Strumble
1971: Mrs Martineau's Jayemji Tanna and Merrymaid of Willowmead
1972: Miss Grattridge's Scapafield Carbon Copy
1973: Miss Galbreath's Carseyhaed Kirsty; Miss Hendry's Sallen Kezia.
1975: Miss Sergeant's Quinbury Wellington Boot; Miss Gallatly's Beckstead Maggie May
1976: Miss Kershaw's Osmart Black Matelot
1977: Mrs Martineau's Jayemji Ruchill and Bailey's Jemma
1978: Miss Yeld's Twyford Majesty; Mr Stanbridge's Yaeger Flair; Mrs Barley's Sallen Rhum; Mrs Buckley's Swinford Sky Flyer
1979: Mrs Morris' Brambledale Bright Spark
1980: Mr Guiver's Becobus Eumenides; Mrs Bartlett's Megifte St Andrews; Mrs Field's Sallen Islay Brown; Mrs Cook's Osmart Angela Black
1981: Miss Gallatly's Peathill Black Sedge; Mrs Kevis' Arranbourne Barabas
1982: Miss Yeld's Tam O'Shagg's Bluff; Mrs Rawson's McDuff's Delinquent; Mrs Prince's Arranbourne Birgitta; Miss Kershaw's Briaridge Crackerjack; Mrs Barley's Quinbury Stormdrifter; Miss Cairns' Cass; Mrs Stafford's Attleford Christmas Rose
1983: Miss Leith's Glencraig Mittened Meg; Mr Nicholl's Jan of Glenfurness; Mrs Ryan's Rags and Ritches of the Glen; Miss Hendry's Lochbarra Black Pandora; Mrs Cook's Potterdale Rhapsody; Miss Morris' Beagold Tosca Hisla
1984: Mrs Robertson's Branault Isle of Canna; Mrs Tonkin's Kensol Deep Mid Winter; Mrs I. Chamberlaine's Arranbourne Black Onyx; Mr Nicholl's Arranbrae Knokandhu; Mr S. Horne's Thomsky Barleycorn Mac; Miss Hill's Alnesaire King Creole; Mr Blackshaw's Alnesaire Johnny Be Good; Miss Bartlett's Scapafield Lingerin' Sunbeam

The Beardie is a member of the working group, and owners should give thought to how they will develop their pets' intelligence. Working capabilities have been bred into every Beardie for generations. It would be tragic if the breed degenerated into merely a beautiful show dog. Several times each year, at Beardie meetings, Working Tests are arranged. Both the Bearded Collie Club and the Southern Counties Bearded Collie Club have approved the composition of these Tests, and there are ample opportunities for any member to qualify for the Club's Diploma or Medal for passing the Senior Test.

The 1978 edition of the notes and regulations is given below:

THE BEARDED COLLIE WORKING TESTS

Approved by both The Bearded Collie Club and the Southern Counties Bearded Collie Club

Revised 1980

1. These tests may be taken only by members of one or the other of Bearded Collie Clubs.
2. The tests are not competitive and to qualify a dog needs to gain 80% of the marks in each exercise.
3. The tests are restricted to Bearded Collies, registered or unregistered. Each dog that qualifies will receive a Diploma from the club running the tests, signed by the judge and a club official. A dog that qualifies in the Senior Test will receive a club medallion.
4. Diplomas will be awarded at the end of the tests. The stewards are responsible for filling in the details on the Diploma and informing the club secretary of the results which will be published in the next edition of the club magazine or newsletter.
5. The club will endeavour to run these tests in any area of the country where there is a minimum of six dogs wanting to qualify.
6. Members wanting a Working Tests meeting in their area must be prepared to find the ground, which shall not belong to any member who is taking part in the meeting. The Junior, Intermediate and Senior Test must take place in the open.
7. Dogs which, without provocation, attack people or other dogs will be disqualified.
8. Bitches in season must not enter the ground. The Handler should inform the judge of the bitch's condition and the judge will examine her after all the other dogs have finished.
9. Members may nominate judges but such names have to be approved by the committee.
10 There must be at least two stewards to assist the judge.
11. Any disputed matter arising at the tests and requiring a decision on the ground will be decided by a majority of the judge, stewards and any officers or committee members of the club running the tests who may be present at the meeting. Their decision shall be final.
12. A dog must have qualified in the Primary Test before taking the Junior, in the Junior Test before taking the Intermediate, and in the Intermediate Test before taking the Senior.

Directions for the guidance of judges
These Working Tests were devised so that the Bearded Collie breed clubs could offer some award for temperamentally sound, well behaved Bearded Collies. The exercises were designed to have a practical aspect and, for this reason, extra commands and encouragement (unless otherwise stated) should not be penalised except where they are excessive and imply lack of control over the dog. The breed standard states that the Bearded Collie should be alert, lively and self-confident with good temperament an essential, and Working Test judges have discretion to penalise the cowed, unwill-

ing worker. The accuracy and precision required for Obedience Competitions are not vital in qualifying for these tests. The dog should be attentive and responsive therefore consistent lagging, wandering or an appreciable delay before responding to a command are faults, whereas minor faults such as the straightness of the sit are not important. The Primary Test has been made very simple to encourage as many people to enter as possible. The Primary and Junior Tests (especially in the lead work) should be judged as assessments of the rapport existing between dog and handler. Great stress has been laid throughout on the dog allowing strangers to examine it. Some adult Bearded Collies are aloof with strangers and this should not be confused with nervousness which must be penalised.

The Primary Test
1. Examination by a stranger. The dog, sitting by the Handler's side, on a loose lead, shall allow itself to be handled by a stranger without showing nervousness or aggression. A change of position by the dog shall not be penalised but backing away through fear will be. Any attempt to bite will disqualify.
                                                        20 points (16 to qualify)
2. The dog to walk on a loose lead beside the Handler, waiting whenever the Handler halts. This shall be done with changes of direction and paces. Distractions will be provided such as a stranger stopping the Handler and talking, another dog on a lead approaching, or clapping by half a dozen people, which should not upset the dog unduly. If the dog barks, the Handler should be able to quieten the dog immediately. This exercise is designed to show whether the dog will accommodate itself to the Handler's pace and direction without pulling on the lead.   20 points (16 to qualify)
3. Recall. The dog shall be held by its collar while the Handler walks some distance away. When called, the dog should come right up to the Handler without any hesitation and have its lead put on. Movement of the Handler towards the dog will be penalised.   20 points (16 to qualify)
4. The dog to be walked on a loose lead within reach of food placed on the ground. The dog should ignore the food when told to do so.   20 points (16 to qualify)
5. Tied stay of one minute. EXTRA COMMANDS ALLOWED. The dog shall be tied to a stake or any other convenient object and the Handler shall walk at least twelve paces away. The dog should not panic, struggle or bark continuously.   20 points (16 to qualify)

The Junior Test
1. Stand for examination, on a loose lead. The Handler can steady the dog as is done in the show ring but the dog should remain standing throughout the examination by the judge.   15 points (12 to qualify)
2. Heelwork on a loose lead, which should incorporate changes of both pace and direction. The dog is expected to sit when the Handler stops.
                                                        15 points (12 to qualify)
3. Recall to handler. The dog may be held by a steward or left in a stay position. When called, the dog should come direct to the Handler and sit in front. No other finish is required.   15 points (12 to qualify)
4. Stay for one minute – extra commands allowed. Handlers will remain in sight and the position that the dog is left in will be at the Handler's discretion. A change of position by the dog will only be penalised slightly but movement away from the spot where it has been left will disqualify. 15 points (12 to qualify)
5. Retrieve any Handler's article. The dog may be held whilst the article is thrown

but should go straight out to pick up the article and deliver it to hand without dropping it. The Handler may give such encouragement as he sees fit.

25 points (20 to qualify)

6. 1 ft. jump off lead. The Handler may jump with the dog if he wished. No slip collars to be worn during jumping. Should the dog fail the jump further attempts are allowed for a loss of two marks for each attempt.

15 points (12 to qualify)

The Intermediate Test

1. Heelwork. A very short stretch of heelwork on the lead is to be immediately followed by a much longer stretch of heel free. The position of the dog to the Handler must be consistent, fairly close, but not impeding the Handler's progress. Changes of pace and direction will be included and the dog should sit when the Handler halts. The same distractions may be provided as in Exercise 2 of the Primary Test.   15 points (12 to qualify)

2. Stay for three minutes – NO EXTRA COMMANDS ALLOWED. Handler's will remain in sight and the position that the dog is left in will be at the Handler's discretion. A change of position by the dog will only be penalised slightly but movement away from the spot where it has been left will disqualify.

15 points (12 to qualify)

3. Recall from the sit or down position to the Handler's side as the Handler is walking away.   15 points (12 to qualify)

4. Stop on recall. The Handler will leave the dog in a stay position recall the animal and stop it on command when it has come part of the way. The Handler will then return to the side of the dog. As this exercise can be a life saver, it is essential that the dog stops immediately on the first command.

10 points (8 to qualify)

5. The dog will jump a 2 ft. hurdle. No slip collars to be worn during jumping. Handlers may run up to the jump to encourage the dog but may not pass the obstacle before the dog does. Should the dog refuse or run out further attempts at the jump are allowed for a loss of two marks for each attempt.

10 points (8 to qualify)

6. The dog will retrieve to hand any article provided by the Handler. The dog is required to go straight out and bring the article straight back without dropping it before the Handler takes it. Any movement of the Handler towards the dog will be penalised.   10 points (8 to qualify)

7. Stand for examination. The dog will be on a loose lead and is required to stand steadily while handled by the judge.   10 points (8 to qualify)

8. *Handler's Choice of:*
Elementary seek back for visible article dropped by the Handler surreptitiously. The dog must be sent back at least fifteen paces and should deliver the article to hand.   15 points (12 to qualify)
Or Elementary Search:
Pieces of 3″ wooden dowelling or garden hose pipe will be provided by the *Organiser* of the tests. The Handler of the dog will have *two* pieces to scent up and then will throw them over his/her's shoulder without the dog seeing them fall. The judge may ask the Handler to take not more than five paces forward before turning and sending the dog to find and deliver to hand *one* article within the time allowed of two minutes. The articles may not be given to the dog before the test commences, or re-used afterwards.   15 points (12 to qualify)

The Senior Test

1. Heel free at fast, slow and normal paces. At one point the dog will be left at either the stand, down or sit at the Handler's command. The Handler will continue as directed by the steward until reaching the dog when both will continue forward together. The dog will be required to remain at heel while its Handler walks through a crowd of people and dogs who are clapping and cheering. Excessive commands by the Handler or barking by the dog, will be penalised. Further distractions may be included at the discretion of the judge. These may include unusual objects and food left on the ground.

   15 points (12 to qualify)

2. Stay in the down position with the Handler out of sight for five minutes – NO EXTRA COMMANDS ALLOWED. A change of position by the dog will only be penalised slightly, but a dog which moves away from the spot on which it was left will be disqualified.   10 points (8 to qualify)

3. *Handler's Choice of:*

   Seek back. With the dog walking at heel, the Handler will surreptitiously drop an article provided by the judge when told to do so. The dog and Handler must proceed at least thirty paces before the dog is sent back to find the article and deliver it to hand. The article should not be smaller than a matchbox, be fairly inconspicuous in colour, and not made of any material likely to cause injury to the dog's mouth. There is a time limit of three minutes from the time the dog is sent to find the article.   15 points (12 to qualify)

   Or:

   A search. The search shall be of an area roughly twelve yards by twelve yards square to find and retrieve one judge's article with Handler's scent placed by a steward unseen by dog and Handler. The Handler may move round the perimeter of the search area but must remain outside it. A separate area must be used for each dog. The time limit is three minutes.   15 points (12 to qualify)

4. Stand for examination off lead. NO EXTRA COMMANDS ALLOWED. The Handler must be at least three foot away.   20 points (16 to qualify)

5. The dog to jump a 5 ft. long jump.   10 points (8 to qualify)

6. The dog to jump a 2′ 6″ hurdle.   10 points (8 to qualify)

   In both 5 and 6 the Handler may run up to the obstacle in order to encourage the dog but must not pass the jump before the dog does. Should the dog fail the jump a further attempt may be made for the loss of two marks. No slip collars to be worn during jumping.

7. The dog to be sent away to a spot marked by its Handler's belongings and dropped beside them. The Handler will return to the spot, pick up the marker, walk away and finally call the dog to heel.   20 points (16 to qualify)

Appendix 3

Breed Clubs and Their Secretaries

The Bearded Collie Club
Miss Beverly Cuddy, Dearbolt Kennels, 802–804 Knowsley Lane, Knowsley Village, Prescot, Merseyside. Telephone 051-546 3644
There are several branches, but information as to their addresses should be obtained from the Secretary of the BCC as they change so often.

Southern Counties Bearded Collie Club
Mrs D. Whitefield, The Lodge, Red House School, Brighton Road, Tadworth, Surrey. Telephone Burgh Heath 58663.

The Bearded Collie Club of Scotland
Mrs M. McVake, 22 Auchenreoch, Milton of Campsie, Glasgow. Telephone 041-775 1200

The Eastern Bearded Collie Association
Mrs Joyce Collis, Peewit House, Astwick Road, Stotfold, Hitchin, Herts. Telephone Hitchin 731077.

Appendix 4

The Kennel Club, 1-4 Clarges Street, London W1Y 8AB

Registration Fees
as from 1st July 1982

	£
Litter Recording by Breeder	
(The total number of puppies must be declared at the time of recording the litter)	
If no puppies named: Litter Recording Fee	5.00
Plus: Each puppy in the litter	1.00 each

e.g. If you have a litter of three dogs and three bitches and you are litter recording only the fee is £5.00 for litter recording, plus £1.00 for each puppy not named. Total £11.00

OR

Litter Recording and Dog Naming by Breeder:
If one or more puppies named:
   Fee £5.00 per puppy named plus £1.00 for each puppy not named in the litter

Three generation pedigree for puppy named	1.00 each

Dog Naming by Owner:

Registration (Salmon Form 2)	5.00
Three Generation Pedigree for dog named (on Salmon Form 2)	2.00
Registration in Obedience Register (Buff Form 1A)	5.00
Change of Name. Affix holders only (Pink Form 8)	5.00

Pedigrees:

Export Pedigrees	20.00
Three Generation Pedigree (not issued at time of Registration or Transfer)	6.00

Transfers:

Transfer by new owner	5.00
Three Generation Pedigree at time of transfer	2.00

These fees are inclusive of VAT at 15%.

All application forms must be accompanied with the appropriate fees and cheques must be crossed payable to the KENNEL CLUB.

If you require any further information or explanations please telephone 01-493 2001.

Index